CHERRINGHAM

A COSY MYSTERY SERIES

MYSTERY AT THE MANOR

Neil Richards • Matthew Costello

RED DOG
UK

Published by RED DOG PRESS 2020

Originally published as an eBook edition by Bastei Lübbe AG,
Cologne, Germany, 2013.

ISBN 978-1-913331-56-6

www.reddogpress.co.uk

Cherringham is a long-running mystery series set in the Cotswolds. The stories are self-contained, though many will enjoy reading them in order of publication:

1.

THE ATTIC

VICTOR HAMBLYN SAT in his easy chair, one gnarled hand locked on a claw armrest, the other holding — none too steady — a glass of sherry in a cut crystal glass.

No matter that the size of the 'pour' seemed minuscule. Victor had other supplies stashed around this draughty castle of a home.

That is — if he could remember where.

Then peeking into the living room, the always cheerful face of Hope, his oh-so-tolerant carer and nurse: "I'm off now, Mr Hamblyn, see you bright and early!"

The sound of her footsteps echoed off the cold stone flags and then he heard the heavy front door slam shut.

He was alone now. He supposed there would come a time when he'd need someone to actually get him to bed, but at ninety-one, amazingly, he wasn't quite there yet and he'd do his best to postpone that final indignity. He took a sip of sherry.

Nice. Not the best, but he could scarcely afford anything near the best, not these days. But, as he often said in his younger days while sipping an inferior gin and tonic at the Raj Club —

it was 'drinkable'.

Of course, back then anything was drinkable, save for the water, which could quite literally kill you. That, and any uncooked food.

Had things changed in India?

Sometimes, he thought about what it was like today. India, the place of his youth, now supposedly an economic powerhouse while the not-so-Great Britain muddled along.

Another sip. Half gone. Simple pleasures. That's what a sherry was. That, and one's memories.

The grandfather clock in the hallway bonged. Still worked, though it had a tendency to lose a few minutes every day. Still that deep, throaty sound! Another simple pleasure.

And with one last sip, he shakily put the glass down. The seat of the chair was high, padded with extra cushions so he could more easily push himself to a standing position.

Two hands on the armrests and…

Success!

And then Victor Hamblyn began a slow navigation to the stairs.

IT HAD BEEN years since he'd actually climbed the great staircase.

Going up now would be hard without the ugly contraption that Hope had insisted must be purchased.

'Those children of yours. You get them to pay, Mr Hamblyn,' she had scolded. 'It isn't decent, you struggling like this.'

And in due course, after the usual bickering the machine had been installed.

Hope had seemed most nervous about leaving him alone to

do this part, but when he demonstrated that he could slide onto the seat of the electric chair and fasten the belt to hold him steady for the ride up, she agreed to depart before he was safely ensconced in his bed.

Now, strapped in good and tight, he hit a button and, with a whirring noise, the chair began ferrying him upstairs.

I could probably do the stairs, he thought, *if I was having a good day, or night.*

Thing is, he never knew whether he'd be having a good day or night. The foolish stair lift was at least dependable.

Riding up, Victor had a good view of the family paintings, all layered with dust on the frames, the paint peeling in places, the colours gloomy with age as sullen generations of Hamblyns from a rosier economic time still found things to scowl about.

The chair stopped, and turned slightly so that Victor could unstrap and slip off. And as he did, he turned on a floor lamp on the landing. He found himself only using the lamp these days rather than the large overhead lights to avoid the jacking up his already frightening electricity bill. As most nights, the thought of a quick visit to his bathroom, and then sliding under the covers, grew ever more appealing with each step.

He slept with the light on. For some reason, it didn't keep him awake at all, and that was even without an eyeshade.

The soft light from the bedside lamp made the gloomy bedroom seem almost warm, even with its tattered carpet, yellowing antimacassars, and the ceiling-high windows that looked over the dark path that led from the village road to the circle just outside the house, now already covered by falling leaves.

Care of the grounds? That too had been let go, with only the minimum being done. A once a month visit by the ground-keeping company was all Victor could afford.

Oh well, he thought. *Not that I ever get out there.*

Then a flash of humour. He could always make people laugh, and even himself.

And he thought… *don't get any leaves inside here!*

He smiled at that, and then felt himself begin to drift off to sleep.

But that drifting, in the soft yellow light of the room, was interrupted, as if he was sliding down a velvety-slope before something pulled him short.

It was a *smell.* He sniffed, as if that could dispel the odour. But it only made the smell seem stronger, and he opened his eyes, realizing with a rush what the smell was.

Fire. Something burning.

And now he struggled to sit, pushing himself up to look around the bedroom.

Nothing here. No fire here. But somewhere in this great house, there was a fire.

He reached for the over-sized mobile phone with a big keypad that was always by his bedside.

He pressed a button — as he had done before, on those other times.

A voice. Then: "It's Victor Hamblyn, in Cherringham, you know, Mogdon Manor and…"

"Yes, Mr Hamblyn we can see it's you. Is there a problem?"

"Yes! A fire!"

"We're on our way. Can you get out of the house?"

He nodded, not realizing for the moment that a nod couldn't be heard.

Because he wasn't thinking of the words being said. He suddenly had only one thought.

He let the phone slide from his fingers, the dispatcher's voice fading as it hit the rumbled sheets and Victor Hamblyn struggled out of bed, even forgetting his slippers as he started for the hall.

OUTSIDE HIS ROOM, small eddies of smoke swirled around. His head pivoted left and right trying to see where all that smoke came from, but he saw no clues. The blackish smoke seemed to be all over, like a stream rising up to his ankles, then higher.

From his vantage point at the top of the stairs, he could see a cascading waterfall of smoke trip its way down to the bottom floor.

But instead of going down the stairs to the door that might lead him to safety, Victor, in as much of a hurry as he could, turned and walked to a door halfway down the hall, pulled out a key from his dressing gown pocket and opened it. Door open, he fumbled for the light.

"God… *damn it!*"

His slow fingers fumbled for a moment but when he hit the switch, a set of bare wooden stairs was illuminated in front of him, leading up to an attic room. Stairs. He hadn't climbed stairs in so long. Now he had to get up to the room, and quickly.

But was that even possible?

Holding firmly on to the thin wooden railing, he placed a bare foot on a step, and then struggled upwards. Like an ancient climber on Everest, he put one foot in front of another and with each torturous step felt his breath getting short, his unused leg muscles aching.

But he kept on going, even when he heard someone, distant and garbled, calling out for him.

'Dad!" Then again, "*Dad!*" Ignoring the voice, Victor kept climbing. There were only a few steps to go, then another door and then a light switch to be found. He'd be there soon. In the distance he could hear more sounds from below: sirens, the fire engines had arrived.

Victor stood at the door and though dizzy with the climb, he was able to turn the knob and enter the room. He blindly batted at the right side of the wall with his hand, and somehow smacked on the light switch.

He stepped into the room. A splinter jabbed into his right foot, but he ignored it.

Up here, the sounds from below had been reduced to just a faint murmur. In the quiet room he looked around, forgetting for a moment where to look, confused because it had been so long since he had been up here.

Where was it? The bright light blinded him and created great long shadows.

"*Where?*" he asked, scared by his own desperation.

The shadows took on a greyish tinge and he found himself coughing. Then a corner of the great attic seemed to vanish in a fog which he quickly realized wasn't fog at all. The smoke had followed him up here.

It rose up beside him, snaking its way into the room, climbing around his legs as he coughed again and again.

The firemen had to be here by now, they would be looking for him in his bedroom. But how long until they came up here?

The coughs constant now, he bent over, an ancient hand covering his mouth. He fell to his knees and then, as whole parts of the room disappeared, there was nothing left for Victor but the fog.

2.

ASHES TO ASHES

SARAH LOOKED OVER at Hope Brown, whose eyes were fixed on the vicar of St James Church as he once again checked his watch. She shivered, regretting having left her winter coat at home. But then she hadn't planned on coming to a funeral this afternoon.

Only a few people stood around the coffin raised near an open grave, in the very corner of the ancient churchyard. A few women, church regulars who probably came to every St James event. They were hardy, these women, thought Sarah. Although the church was in the centre of the village, the autumn winds seemed always to find it, and the big old yew tree rustled constantly.

"For God's sake," the man next to her muttered under his breath. Sarah knew him of old: one of Victor Hamblyn's sons, Dominic. In his early fifties, Dominic had a long reputation in the village as someone who splashed the cash.

At the height of the boom he'd been all champagne and fifty-pound notes. From the slightly orange tone of his face, thought Sarah, these days it seemed he concentrated on his tan...

Next to him, his wife Vanessa — co-owner of Coole

Solutions, the village's supposedly trendy and certainly pricey interior design shop. She wore the wide-eyed look of someone who would explode if she spent another minute here.

On the opposite side of the grave from Dominic and his wife, Sarah saw Susan Hamblyn, wearing a crisp grey suit, looking every bit the tough accountant. During the brief church service Sarah had been amazed to see her using her phone, probably writing emails.

And next to Sarah, the last member of the little cluster around the grave — her own friend Hope. Sarah caught her eye and Hope rolled her eyes as if to say *see what I have to put up with?*

At the last minute, Sarah had volunteered to accompany Hope, Victor's carer, to the old man's funeral.

Hope had checked in on him three times a day and had grown to like the old man.

"He was strange, odd in his ways, you know?" she'd once told Sarah. "But there was something sweet there, too."

On the subject of his offspring and their infrequent visits, Hope had nothing good to say.

Hope, Sarah knew all too well, didn't easily indulge in judgements. But her silence now spoke volumes.

Another gust of wind blew swirls of leaves through the weathered gravestones. Everyone was now waiting for offspring number three.

Hope gave Sarah's left hand a quick squeeze. "Thank you for coming, Sarah." She said quietly. "Didn't know we'd have such a long wait."

"No worries," Sarah replied. At least the day was cooperating — just. Clouds threatening rain but so far it was still dry.

Finally, Reverend Hewitt shook his head.

8

"I'm afraid, well, we really can't wait any longer. I have a wedding at East Charlton so… Best, I begin, yes?"

The vicar, all thick glasses that matched his black hair tousled by the wind, was as exciting in making this decision as he was when Sarah heard him sermonizing.

A gentle man, with a quiet owl-eyed wife who organized occasional afternoon teas at the vicarage, they were as mild and meek as one could ask for.

"Yes," Dominic said, catching matching glares from his sister and wife. "We all have things to *do*. And Terry, well you know Terry…"

Then, as if on cue, Terry walked over.

In fact he wobbled, obviously having fortified himself for his father's internment with an early liquid breakfast at the Railway Arms.

And he'd even dressed for the occasion, with a black-and-white Metallica T-shirt stretched over his expansive belly.

Sarah guessed that Terry's wardrobe choices back at his caravan were limited.

But now that he had arrived, it was time for the final act of the show to start.

First Susan. "So *good* of you to come, Terry."

Dominic also showed an inability to restrain his commentary on Terry's late arrival: "Can't even be on time for your own father's bloody funeral?"

Terry swayed slightly as if the rebukes were wind gusts sending him bobbing left and right. Then he recovered his stance.

"Right. Sure. *You'se lot*… as if you cared for the old sod… one…" he paused, perhaps realizing that the vicar was watching, missal in hand. Sarah looked at Hope, thinking that the sweet nurse probably hadn't bargained on a show like this.

But then, maybe she had seen similar, or even worse, when Victor's family gathered at the decrepit manor.

"… not one… *bit*." Terry continued. "Just got your greedy damn eyes on the Manor, the property, huh, huh?" He looked around wildly at his siblings.

"Please." Reverend Hewitt held up a hand as if he might part the waves of acrimony now surrounding the shiny wooden coffin. "Out of respect," he said, looking at the remaining Hamblyn members.

Hope looked over at Sarah; perhaps, Sarah thought, she was suddenly feeling that this was too much to ask of a friend. But Sarah gave her a bright smile back. And thought: *I decided to come back to the village, to live a village life. And this, standing with a friend, is part of that.*

Despite the vicar's plea, Terry had one more riposte. "Nothing to say, do you? Nothing!" Then he straightened up as best he could and gave the vicar a drunken wave of his hand signalling that the ceremony could finally begin.

Reverend Hewitt nodded. His white surplice flapped in the wind. He opened up the missal and then, with a gentle clearing of his throat, began…

"Dear friends, family — a reading from Isaiah 25… 'He will swallow up death in victory; and the Lord God will wipe away tears from off all faces; and the rebuke of his people shall he take away from all the earth: for the Lord hath spoken it!'"

And then — the first drops of rain.

It, too, had waited long enough.

"Sarah, thank you *so* much for coming."

Hope, ever resourceful, had brought a large enough umbrella to shelter them both from what had turned into a steady downpour.

Over her friend's shoulder, she could see workmen with

shovels preparing to cover up the grave.

"No worries. I got to see the Hamblyn family in action, didn't I? They are *quite* a family."

Hope nodded, looked away, and then back at Susan.

"There's something I wanted to mention to you." Hope chewed her lips and Sarah couldn't imagine what had her looking so serious.

"Of course."

"I mean, I know you're friends with that American, from New York." A pause. "The detective."

"*Retired* detective."

"Yes. But here's the thing, Sarah…"

It helped that they were huddled under the umbrella, making the conspiratorial whispering look not so conspiratorial. "The night Victor died…"

Sarah nodded.

"You see, they found him in a room that he told me no one was ever to enter, way up in the attic. No one, *ever*. He said that if any of his family visited and I was in the house, I had to make sure they never went up there."

With a small smile, Hope looked over at the grave to where Victor's children had just been standing.

"Though how I was supposed to do that was anybody's guess."

"A forbidden room, then?" Sarah said.

"Yes."

"And do you know what secret was in that room?"

"No. You know me, Sarah. Never asked and he never told. But I have to tell you this…"

Hope's umbrella, the size of a small tent, was doing a good job of keeping the heavy rain off them.

"I never — *ever* — in all my years looking after him so much as saw him look at the door leading up there. Only — once in a while, especially if he'd sneaked an extra sherry or two — he'd stare right at me and repeat that no one must ever go up there. I'd say, of course, you already told me…"

"Did he mean… even after he died?"

"Possibly. Some hope with that fine lot of kids prowling over the place."

"Interesting," Sarah said. "I can imagine they're all itching to scour the house."

Another mystery, she thought. Cherringham was turning out to be more mysterious than she would have ever expected.

But she also sensed as Hope stood there, her face set, eyes narrow, a worried look — that there was more.

"Sarah, I think there's something wrong here. The fire, Victor going upstairs when he should have been trying to get out of the house, going up where I never saw him go."

Hope took a breath.

"Something's *wrong.*"

Sarah, not sure she agreed, nodded.

Things happened in life.

She knew that well. Married with kids one day, the next a single mum back in her home village. *Life is full of surprises,* she thought.

Hope reached out and grabbed Sarah's free hand.

"Can you ask your friend? To look into it."

"Gosh Hope — I don't…"

A squeeze. "Please, Sarah. You know I'd never normally ask but Victor was such a sweet old man. A little strange perhaps, a bit poor — but I just feel like something's not right here." A gust of wind sent rain flying in under the protection of the umbrella.

"Can you?"

Sarah looked at the grave in the far corner, the workmen shovelling heavy black earth. Victor Hamblyn just another resident in a place where — what was her father's corny joke? — everyone's dying to get in.

Victor Hamblyn was gone. But if Hope was right, a mystery remained.

"Okay. I'll talk to him, and see what he thinks."

Now, a full on smile from Hope. "Thank you. I won't forget this Sarah."

Another gust, more rain spatters. "And we'd better get indoors. Do you want to come up to the office for a cuppa?"

Sarah nodded, and together they walked round the corner and into the village square.

3.

AN UNFORTUNATE ACCIDENT

SARAH KNOCKED ON the door of the 'Grey Goose', Jack's river barge. A gentle rap at first, but then harder.

"Jack? You in there?"

She hadn't seen much of him, what with the past few weeks being so busy — just a quick hello as they passed at the Saturday market or the newsagents. Jack had gone back to being the quiet, invisible ex-pat.

Then a louder rap. "Jack?"

Finally she heard a growl — his dog, Riley — and then steps.

Jack opened the door dressed in rumpled cargo shorts and a frayed Hawaiian Smokin' Joe's T-shirt. A volcano sat above words that promised 'air-conditioning and the best place to return any cursed lava rocks you might have picked up'.

Guess the volcano gods weren't to be trifled with, she thought.

Though mid-morning, Jack had obviously just woken up and Sarah found herself wondering whether it was because he'd had a late night, or whether he'd stayed awake thinking about the past.

She should drop in more, she thought. People, even former

NYPD detectives, can vanish into their own hidey-holes.

"Sarah, um…"

"Sorry for waking you."

Jack smiled, the lines on his face receding. "No worries. Should have gotten up earlier. Stayed up a bit last night. Reading."

Sarah nodded. Jack could be quiet, and she knew best not to dig deep.

"Got a minute? Something I'd like to talk to you about."

His smile broadened. "Oh, do you? Let me guess, is something, as your great Mr Conan Doyle might write, *afoot*?"

"Could be."

"Then let me get the kettle on — see, I am picking up the ways of you natives here — and we'll talk."

But Riley stuck his snout in the door, and looked left and right.

"Er, Jack — maybe Riley needs a walk first."

"Right. Okay. Walk the dog, then the kettle. Going to be a bit mushy out there. You coming?"

Jack reached to the side of the open door, grabbed Riley's leash, and clipped it to the dog's collar before pulling on his boots. Sarah followed, as the dog led the way out to the meadow that sprawled from the riverfront, away from the barges and boats.

Jack soon let Riley run free through the meadow. An occasional gull swooped down, and dog and bird almost seemed to be playing a game of tag.

Stayed up reading? Jack thought.

True, he loved to get lost in his history books but last night, there was too much Brooklyn, too much Katherine, too many memories floating around to get lost in his new history of Stalingrad.

But now the morning air felt good, clearing cobwebs.

And seeing Sarah? Always good. Although she had two devoted parents right in the village, Jack felt something he could only describe as fatherly concern for her. Raising a family on your own was always tough.

As Riley dashed, Jack turned to Sarah.

"So your friend says that the old man never went up to this room. And yet, a fire breaks out and up he goes? Or maybe he was already there?"

"Yes."

"Maybe he was already up there?"

"Possible. But why? In the middle of the night?"

"Right." He looked away. Riley had stopped, his nose pointed straight into the air at the taunting gull. A lot of thoughts swirled in Jack's head. He had dealt with a lot of suspicious fires in his days in New York. Some were simply fires — things happen — and some weren't.

He turned back to Sarah.

"What do you think?" she said.

"I'm guessing you're asking me if I want to play detective again?"

"Well, not sure if 'play' is the right word, after all, I've seen all those plaques and commendations — you must have done *something* for them."

He held up a hand, laughing. "Okay. Well, on first glance what you're telling me is interesting. Still — it could be nothing. Old people do odd things — for lots of reasons. Maybe he thought he was going downstairs."

"And maybe he knew exactly where he was going."

"You are the suspicious one, aren't you?" He took a breath. "I like that."

"If you'd seen the show put on by his family..."

16

"The ne'er-do-well offspring, hmm?"

"Accusations flying, all of them looking relieved that their dad was in the ground."

Jack nodded. "Okay. I'm in. Or rather, *we're* in. A team, yes?"

"Of course. Though I need to do a bit of work — just blew the whole morning and I have a highlands resort waiting on a layout for their brochure and website. But after that…"

"And I need that cup of tea."

"Where do we start?"

"You know… some people will talk to us, some people won't. And since this is a fire matter, how about we start with your Fire Department and the Fire Chief? That what you call them here?"

She laughed at the question. "It's called the Fire and Rescue Service, and we have a Chief Fire Officer Barnes."

"There you go. Not so different. Let's have a chat with him — if he will chat. When can you be free?"

"Half-two, three?"

He grinned. Slowly, the expressions here were becoming normal. *Half-two.*

"Great. Saw the fire station out towards the school."

"Brand new, almost."

"Meet you there not at half-two but, say… two-thirty?"

And now Sarah grinned.

SARAH SAW CHIEF Fire Officer Barnes standing outside the station as his men washed a bright red fire engine lined with yellow stripes.

She looked at her watch. Half-two, and no Jack.

Then she heard his Austin-Healey Sprite take the corner

near the station, the engine's low rumble more distinctive than even its vintage sports car profile.

She popped the door as Jack parked across the street and twisted and turned his way out of the driver's seat.

He really needs a bigger car, she thought.

He had put on khakis, a crisp blue shirt, his rumpled morning look gone.

"You want to start?" he said quietly as they got closer to Barnes who had seen them.

"As long as I can pass it to you. What I know about arson could fill the back of a postage stamp."

The Chief took a few steps towards them.

"Sarah Edwards?"

"Chief Barnes."

The Chief Fire Officer wore a smile.

Had he heard about how Sarah had helped find Sammi's killer back in the summer? If so, he might know what she was doing here.

"Your dad told me at the Parish Council meeting a few months ago that you were back. Missed the old village life?"

She waited for the next bit, the part that always seemed laced with an air of judgement.

"And two kids as well, hmm?"

Sarah nodded. She fired a quick look at Jack, who stood there taking little interest in this chit-chat, instead watching the men hosing down the fire engine.

Sarah hoped he might step in and redirect the conversation. But no such luck.

"Yup — Chloe and Daniel."

"Yes, watched your boy play cricket last weekend. Kid's got some real skills."

Sarah smiled, this loop of chit-chat feeling interminable.

Finally Jack intervened. "Jack Brennan," he said sticking his hand out.

With an unhidden sense of caution, Barnes offered his hand and gave Jack's a firm shake.

But at least it stopped the 'catching-up' train.

"Chief, my good friend Hope was Victor Hamblyn's carer."

From the corner of her eye she caught a fireman nearby looking over, still polishing the engine which already looked as shiny and bright as possible.

Barnes nodded, and also folded his arms, the body language clear.

Sarah continued. "She thought that there was something wrong, about the fire and…"

Barnes unfolded his arms and put a hand out as if directing traffic.

"Now hang on, Sarah. I can't talk about that incident, an unfortunate accident. There'll be an inquest in due course, and until then I can't say anything."

Sarah nodded. She watched as Barnes looked over to Jack as if expecting an argument there.

"I know," Sarah said, searching for words that might make this by-the-book Fire Chief bend the rules just a bit. "But Hope, she told me…"

Barnes shook his head. "If your friend has any information, I suggest she pass that along. We'll be working with the police on the incident and will be glad to look at anything."

Sarah felt the heavy virtual thud of a door slamming shut.

She looked at Jack, as if to say… *c'mon, nothing to say here? No magic words from the New York detective to rock the Chief's boots a bit?*

"Makes sense," was all that Jack said.

Sarah thinking… *good grief.*

"Okay," Sarah said. "I'll make sure she does that."

Chief Barnes smiled. "Good. And I'd better see to my desk. Love fighting fires, hate the paperwork!"

Barnes turned and walked away.

Sarah turned to Jack who signalled with a nod of his head that they should move on, but they had only taken a few steps before Sarah felt someone touch her elbow.

4.

SMOKE AND FIRE

SARAH TURNED AROUND, with Jack, and saw one of the firemen, his uniform dotted with water from the engine cleaning, standing there.

"Excuse me," he said. He sounded breathless, whether from dashing to catch them or from whatever had prompted him to drop his soapy rag and follow them.

She saw the fireman look back to the station house but no one seemed to be watching.

Jack's eyes were locked on the young fireman. The nametag above the pocket of his shirt: *Gary Scott.*

"Yes?"

"I—I couldn't help hear what you two were talking about back there. I know Hope. She took care of my gran, very near the end. A big heart, she has."

"She does," Sarah said.

"My family owed her. Could have been a bad experience. Know what I mean? But Hope, was, well like really special."

Nothing important here, Sarah thought. Just a thanks to pass along to the gentle, caring Hope — who would of course dismiss the compliment, saying she just did what anyone would do.

Sarah smiled, ready to go back to her car, and talk with Jack to see what else they could look into when the young man, with a quick glance behind him, leaned forward to say something more.

"I heard your question." He said quietly. "If Hope is concerned, I dunno, maybe something *was* wrong there."

Which is when Jack spoke. "Did you see something? That night?"

The fireman nodded. "This last year, we've been out to the Manor a lot. Hope probably knows that. The wiring in that place was a mess. Decades overdue for an upgrade. So little electrical fires started all the time. Every month nearly. Think she called in one or two of them. But mostly the old man. He was old, you know, but sharp."

"So, it wasn't the first night you'd been to the house?" said Jack.

Gary Scott nodded. "Right. And, truth be known, the place was ripe for fires. Should have been condemned, least till the wiring was upgraded."

"Anything else?" Sarah said. She was concerned that Barnes might emerge from the station again, and the young fireman would get in trouble for his help.

"Well, I don't know if you know anything about electrical fires. Usually start in the wall, often near the sockets. Can take a while for them to turn into anything. Even in those old places, the wires were kept free of exposed wood, the walls."

"Something strange about this one?"

Another nod. "Yes and no. The fire started in the old library. There were no traces of accelerant we could see."

"Accelerant?" said Sarah.

"Lighter fluid, petrol — you know? Deliberate stuff," said

Gary. "Anyway, far as I know, that room never got used by Mr Hamblyn. Whereas the other call-outs we had — it was in the living areas. But what really struck me was the old fella being right at the top of the house. I mean — he had to use a stair lift just to get to bed! Whatever he was up to — he was desperate. Know what I mean?"

Sarah shot another look at Jack. Though a warmish sun beat down on them, hearing Gary's words chilled her. And she knew: Hope's instincts were spot on.

"Maybe he was just disorientated?" she said.

"Nah. Sharp as nails old Victor was. He knew the way out in a fire." He looked over his shoulder again. "Anyway, I'd better go. Chief will have my head if he catches me with you. But one other thing. That night, when we got there, we saw someone near the house."

"Running from the house or…?" Jack said.

Gary shook his head. "No. Just like — standing there. Like they wanted to go in. Maybe someone out for a walk. The pub's not far. But as soon as we rolled up…"

"They ran away?" Jack said.

Gary looked at Jack. "Exactly. And we had our hands full. And by the time we were suited up, tanks, masks, and inside — it was too late for the old man."

"Can't have been pleasant," said Jack.

Gary shook his head. "Never is. But he wouldn't have known much about it. Smoke, you see. His age — coupla deep breaths, that's all it takes. Anyway. Gotta go. Wish you guys luck."

He turned, ready to bolt back, but then:

"Good you two are out asking questions. This lot here," a thumb arched in the direction of the station house, "they do take their time!"

A last grin, and Gary Scott hustled back to the gleaming fire truck drying in the afternoon sun.

Sarah turned to Jack.

"So, what do you think?"

Jack nodded at her, clearly thinking this through.

"I think I should pay a visit to the mystery manor — don't you?"

And Sarah knew she'd got him on board.

5.

THE ROOM IN THE ATTIC

JACK DROVE SLOWLY up the road from Cherringham Bridge towards the village, peering through the misted-up windows of the little sports car, looking for the entrance to Mogdon Manor.

He'd walked up this gentle hill many times, but had no idea that one of the little lanes off the main road led to one of the oldest houses in the area. Barely visible through the overgrown hedges, two crumbling stone gate pillars stood beneath a rusty iron arch with faded lettering — *Mogdon Manor*.

He turned in to the weed-covered drive and followed it, brambles and shrubs brushing the sides of the car. As he rounded a corner the hedges opened out and the house appeared, set behind a circle of gravel and an ornamental fountain that had probably at one stage been very grand.

As he climbed out of the car, he took stock of the place. Through the rain, the house looked to Jack like it should be in a horror movie. Broad and squat, the old building was smothered in ivy and the skeletal branches of an ancient wisteria. Dark leaded windows set in ancient stone, a heavy oak front door with iron studs, and a stone tiled roof from which floods of water cascaded noisily down where broken guttering hung loose.

Behind it, towered four great oak trees — Jack guessed that even on a sunny day the house would be in almost constant shadow.

But as far as he could see, there was no trace of the fire that had caused Victor Hamblyn's death.

As he took it all in, a little Fiat buzzed up the drive and parked next to the Sprite. A woman got out, umbrella already flicking open. She rushed over to him and took him by the arm.

"Come on love," she said. "We'll catch our deaths out here."

And before he could even speak, Hope Brown led him round to the side of the house, unlocked a back door, and bustled him in.

As she put the kettle on and proceeded to make coffee, she turned to Jack. "Of course, I could have just given Sarah the key and left the two of you to it. But to be honest — I really wanted to meet you. Up close and personal — isn't that what you Yanks say?"

Jack considered his reply carefully.

"Not too up close, I hope. These days the lines are pretty much all you'll see."

"Nonsense. Laughter lines. Sign of experience. A rich, full life and all that."

"A long one — that's what it feels like most mornings," said Jack.

She handed him his coffee and took a seat on the other side of the kitchen bar and examined him. Jack examined back. She was in her late thirties he guessed — a little older than Sarah. Fuller figure, strong-looking, and a lot of laughter in those eyes for sure.

He liked her instantly. No wonder Gary up at the Fire Station had so much time for her.

"This kitchen," he said. "In a manor house like this it seems kinda incongruous, don't you think?"

He nodded towards the state-of-the-art oven and double fridge, the smooth granite worktops, professional lighting.

"Total waste of money if you ask me," said Hope. "Dominic had it all installed in the spring. Insisted on it. 'Only the best is good enough for you, Dad.' Getting him that stair lift? *That* was a different matter, mind you."

"And what did *Dad* think about all this?"

"He used to come in, make his tea, use the toaster — swear a bit at the expense, then go back to his little sitting room."

"So he wasn't impressed with son's generosity?"

"He thought Dominic was a complete waster. Spent money when he had it, spent even more when he didn't."

"And what do you think?"

"Ah, Mr Detective you won't catch me out like that," she said, eyes twinkling. "I was Victor's carer. He knew how I felt about them."

"So you did have an opinion then?" said Jack, sipping his coffee.

Hope smiled at that.

Yes, he definitely liked her.

"Let me show you round," she said, ignoring his question. "Come on — we'll do the grand tour. Bring your coffee — it'll be cold by the time we get back here."

The kitchen was at the side of the house, at one end of a long, cold corridor. Jack followed as Hope worked what sounded like an estate agent's spiel, opening and closing doors. Jack was immediately aware of the acrid smell of burnt wood and plastic that hung in the corridor.

"Downstairs bathroom. Note the original Victorian plumbing. Cellar with a lovely rich smell of damp. Laundry room — not used for twenty years, watch out for moths, spiders and who knows what else. And the library, which is where the fire started…"

Hope opened the door — but went no further, and Jack could see — and smell — why. The room was lined with charred, blackened bookshelves. The walls and curtains had all burned away. The floor was scattered with sodden debris, piles of blackened books and damaged furniture. The air was even worse here and caught in the back of his throat.

"Over there — that's the socket where they think the wiring caught," said Hope.

Jack could see where the firemen had axed their way into the wall, ripping out the skirting boards to access the source of the fire.

"Did Victor ever use this room?" said Jack.

"Not that I can remember. Used to stay in his little sitting room down the hallway. He would ask me to get a book for him sometimes — he never came in here himself."

"So why would that socket suddenly start a fire?"

"Exactly, Inspector: why indeed?"

Jack gave the room a final scan. On an ornate trunk by the window, sat a large bronze elephant statue, with incongruous arms looping from its body. It was familiar — Indian — was it a god? And now as he looked more carefully, he could see other Indian artefacts in the burned wreckage — lacquered cabinets, pewter pots, faded group photos in blackened frames.

"What's with all the Indian stuff?" he said.

"House is full of it," she said, shrugging slightly. "Victor lived out there when he was younger."

"During the Second World War?"

"Slightly later, I think. But he never talked about it. Well, not to me, anyway."

Hope closed the blackened door and nodded towards the hallway.

"The tour continues…"

Jack followed her down the stone-floored corridor and into the main hallway. Although the smell of smoke was still strong, there wasn't as much damage.

"So the fire wasn't so bad down here?" he said.

"Fire brigade got here pretty quickly, I think," said Hope. "It's the smoke that's the killer. Streamed straight to the attic, like a chimney, trapping Victor."

"If he had been down here… he'd still be alive."

"Yes. There was quite a lot of water from the hoses, and smoke marks on the walls — but it's only the library that really got damaged."

"So this is pretty much how it was after the fire?"

"There was a right mess everywhere. But I mopped up, and cleaned all the surfaces I could — just to get rid of the smell, really."

Jack looked around. Things were not adding up here. Then:

"Where was Victor when the fire broke out?" said Jack.

"Up in his bedroom I reckon," said Hope, heading to the staircase. "His bed was slept in. And he'd had his biscuits — I always leave him a couple."

"Usual routine, huh?"

"Exactly. You see the lift is still up at the top?"

"Maybe he felt it was safer to stay upstairs?"

"He may have been frail, but he wasn't stupid," said Hope, shaking her head. "He knew not to go upstairs in a fire."

She nodded and headed to the next floor.

Jack followed her to the staircase. Rails for an electric stair lift ran all along one side. As he and Hope walked up to the first floor, the smell of smoke permeated.

Hope paused at the top and pointed down the landing.

"Victor's bedroom and bathroom are just there."

She pointed the other way, down a long dark corridor, its walls covered in oak panelling.

"Those are the other bedrooms. All closed and locked up."

"Not used at all? No guests? No family to stay?"

"Not one — at least, not in the three years I've been looking after him."

"So where are the stairs to the top floor? If he went up, not down..."

"I thought you'd never ask," said Hope, drawing a key from her pocket.

Jack watched as she walked a few paces to a small door set back in the panelling, turned the key and pushed the door open to reveal a narrow flight of stairs.

"These go up to the attic."

"Locked staircase, huh? What's the point of that?"

"Beats me. I always thought it just went to the old servants' quarters — and they didn't want a staircase to spoil the effect of the panelling. So, just this door."

"It's pretty steep," said Jack, peering up into the darkness above. "I mean, for someone who uses an electric chair."

"Exactly," said Hope. "Put yourself in Victor's shoes. He smells smoke, comes out onto the landing here — and instead of going down on the stair lift..."

"He unlocks this door and climbs a steep flight of stairs," said Jack. "But — dunno — maybe in the night, in the dark, in smoke, people make bad choices."

Hope shook her head. "Victor *always* knew what he was doing."

"Trust me," she flicked on the electric light to the stairs, "If Victor Hamblyn came up here — he had a very good reason."

6.

ROOM AT THE TOP

JACK FOLLOWED HOPE up the narrow staircase. A door at the top opened into a big attic room in the eaves, lit by a tiny leaded skylight. Jack stooped under the low roof and looked around, his eyes adjusting to the dim light. The place was full of dust and cobwebs — but apart from that, it was completely empty.

That did make him pause.

And for the first time Jack began to feel that maybe there really was a mystery about this old man's death. Did he go upstairs to escape the smoke? Or for another reason?

He turned — to see Hope standing in the doorway behind him, expression now serious.

"Where was his body found?" he said.

"Lying there, apparently," she answered. "In the middle of the floor."

Jack nodded. Carefully he scanned the whole room. Dust everywhere. Scuffs and marks on the floor where medics, firemen had obviously been. Thick clouds of cobwebs hung in every corner. The walls were bare, the window rusted shut.

Nothing here.

It didn't make sense.

"Well, now you got me," he said, turning to face her. "You say he wouldn't allow anyone to come up here?"

"No. And he kept the key. The only key — as far as I know. It was in the door downstairs, so I took it when I came in to clean up."

"Maybe he found what he was looking for?"

"The police returned his pyjamas and dressing gown. He had nothing in the pockets."

Jack frowned.

"Maybe…"

From within the house below came a low animal groan and the sound of glass smashing. Hope turned to him.

"What was that?" she whispered.

Jack put a finger to his lips.

"Who else has a key to this place?" said Jack quietly.

"No one, as far as I know," said Hope. "Victor refused to have other keys made."

"Okay. Stay behind me — let's go see."

Jack tiptoed down the attic stairs, wincing when the dry wood gave even his careful steps a tell-tale creak.

When he got to the bottom, he stopped and listened carefully to the noises of the house. From the ground floor came the sound of objects being moved, voices, swearing.

He went down the main stairs but then stopped: the disturbance was in Victor's sitting room. Jack gestured to Hope to stay where she was, then as quietly as he could, he approached the door.

There were two ways of doing this — the slow way or the quick way. He'd always been a fan of the quick way.

Guessing the door wasn't locked, Jack grabbed the door handle, pushing it hard and bursting into the room. The light was on — and facing him, Jack saw a long-haired man in an old vest and jeans, holding a bottle and surrounded by piles of clothes and books and boxes. The man spun around, shouted and swung the bottle wildly at Jack.

Jack easily sidestepped the swing and hit the intruder hard with his shoulder, knocking him straight over, then expertly flipped him and instinctively reached behind his back for his cuffs and felt just thin air...

... because his NYPD cuffs hadn't been strapped to his belt for at least five years.

In this case it didn't matter. The guy had given up — *lucky for me*, thought Jack — and now stammered a drunken protest.

"Let me go! I haven't done anything. You can't arrest me!"

"Terry!" came Hope's voice from the doorway. "What are you doing here?"

"You know this guy?" said Jack over his shoulder.

"It's Terry Hamblyn," said Hope. "Victor's son."

And Jack released his grip.

"YOU HURT MY arm," said Terry, sullenly. "I should sue you."

Jack stared at Terry, the youngest of the Hamblyn siblings, as he sat in Victor's battered armchair and clutched the mug of coffee which Hope had made as a peace offering.

"Sure. Go ahead," said Jack. "But mind — when we get to court, I'll be asking just how you got access to your father's house and why you were tearing the place apart."

"It's my house, isn't it?" said Terry. "I can do what I want."

Jack leaned against the fireplace and watched Terry carefully. He was up to no good — but what exactly? The guy had clearly spent many years boozing — probably drugs too — and now he flickered between irrational and incoherent.

"I'm not sure that it is your house, least not yet. There's a little matter of a will," said Jack.

"Course it is! He was my dad!"

"With respect, Terry," said Hope, who sat in the chair opposite, "Your father not only took your keys away months ago, he told me never to let you in if he wasn't here himself."

"That's rubbish," said Terry sneering. "Dad and I were best mates. He was going to leave the whole place to me. No question."

"Really? Doesn't mean you can just break in and take stuff, Terry," said Jack. "You see, I'm sure there's a whole process that has to be followed. And what about your brother and sister?"

"Those bastards? He *hated* them."

"From what I hear, they did at least help out with the place," said Jack.

"Bollocks. They were just getting their fingers in the pie."

"Oh? How so?"

"Obvious, isn't it?" said Terry. "Dominic — he was doing up the kitchen how that bitch of a wife of his wanted it so they could move in when the old man popped his clogs."

"And what about your sister?"

"Smarmy Susan? She had Dad's accounts all sorted so she knew exactly what he was worth. She had big plans."

"But you get the house, huh?" said Jack.

Terry grinned.

"Yeah, that'll teach them."

"So — bear with me, I'm a little confused — if you're going to get the house, why come round here searching for stuff?"

Terry's bloodshot eyes went wide.

"What do you mean, searching? I just came round to have a bit of a kip. Then you turn up and wake me. I wasn't searching

34

for anything."

Jack gestured to the mess of the room. The drawers had been roughly pulled out of every cupboard and their contents tipped out in piles.

"Well, you certainly weren't tidying the place up, Terry," said Jack patiently. "What exactly were you looking for?"

"Nothing! Family stuff, that's all. Private stuff!"

"And you weren't round here the night of the fire?" continued Jack. "You weren't outside, watching?"

"No way! That wasn't me! I had nothing to do with it!"

"Oh," said Jack. "So — you think the fire was started deliberately?"

Jack could see confusion clouding Terry's mind.

"No! Yes. I don't know."

Jack watched as Terry slowly decided that it was time to leave. He pulled himself up unsteadily from the chair.

"Anyway, you can't keep me here. I know my rights!"

Jack caught Hope's eye and held back a smile.

"I'm sure you do, Terry," he said. "We're just having a chat, aren't we?"

"Not anymore we're not," said Terry, picking up a battered leather coat from the floor and headed to the door. He pulled it open and turned dramatically.

"I loved my dad. And he loved me," he said, swaying slightly. "And if you think someone killed him — it's my bastard brother and sister you should be talking to." Terry sniffed as if suddenly righteous, and then: "And what are you's two doing here?"

Hope's voice was level, steady: "Your father gave me a key. Said to use it anytime."

Terry gave another snort and with that, he was gone. Jack turned to Hope, who sat, arms folded, watching the door.

"Know what?" he said. "If Victor was murdered — then it's you who should be prime suspect."

"Oh really?" said Hope, not following. "Why?"

"Because nobody could put up with this family for three years and not want to frame them."

Hope smiled. "It's a fair cop." She looked around at the mess. "Then we'd better lock up and go before you arrest me. And don't forget — I've now seen you in action."

Jack laughed.

"Please, don't tell anybody," he said. "I'm well out of practice."

"Looked pretty slick to me."

And Jack thought — heck, maybe there is life in this old dog yet.

7.

A TRIP INTO TOWN

SARAH SAT IN the busy reception area of Davies Associates and looked out through the window and down onto the High Street.

Although Oxford was just half an hour on the train from Cherringham, she very rarely visited — and especially not since weekends had filled up so much with activities for the children. But this morning's outing had reminded her how much she loved the city.

She'd left Grace in charge of the office at nine and by ten she was drinking coffee in the Ashmolean. Two wonderful hours of gallery viewing later she was trying on shoes in a little designer store off Walton Street, followed by lunch in her favourite fish restaurant then another coffee in the bustling little covered market just up from Carfax.

All in all it felt like being on holiday. Until now.

The clinical atmosphere of a corporate tax advisors would be enough to dampen even her son Daniel's sense of fun.

She looked around the discreetly designed wood panelled room, with its marble floor and matt steel trim. The plaque behind reception listed all the partners who worked in the company — and Susan Hamblyn's name was almost at the top of the list.

On the walls were large photos of commercial property developments around the world: so this was what Victor's prim daughter did — raise finances for slick hotels.

A light flickered on the immaculate receptionist's desk phone. The ice maiden picked it up, murmured an answer then put the phone down. She gave Sarah a tight-lipped smile.

"Ms Hamblyn will see you now. Third floor. Someone will meet you."

Sarah gathered up her shopping bags and, suddenly feeling like a real country bumpkin, made her way to the lift.

"You'll have to forgive me, Mrs Edwards, but I've had to reshuffle my meetings this afternoon and I can only give you fifteen minutes."

Sarah sat in the informal sofa area of Susan Hamblyn's office and felt anything but informal.

"I'm sure fifteen minutes will be ample."

The accountant shrugged. "My apologies."

Sarah knew an apology when it wasn't one. Susan Hamblyn hadn't wanted to meet a web designer from Cherringham, but Sarah had insisted on the phone that she had some important and personal matters to discuss related to her father.

That had obviously been enough to pique the woman's interest and get this brief meeting.

Right now she was wishing that she'd taken Jack's suggestion and met the brother not the sister — but when they'd tossed a coin, this was the interview she'd got so she'd stuck with the rules.

Susan folded her arms, her perfectly cut business suit not moving a centimetre out of shape.

"You said you had important information about my father's

death. I'd like to know what that information is — and why you have it."

Sarah refused to be intimidated.

Back in London I used to deal with people like this all the time, she thought — *and I still can.*

"Of course," she said, smiling generously. "I appreciate you taking the time to see me — I realize what a busy woman you must be."

Another curt nod. "Go on."

"I've been approached by somebody — whose name I cannot reveal — who is very concerned that the recent fire at Mogdon Manor may have been started deliberately. And that your father's death may not be accidental."

"I see."

Sarah let the words hang in the air a moment. Then:

"I thought I should meet with you and get your opinion."

"And what right do you have to go around investigating rumours about people you have neither met nor know?"

"I'm simply trying to help a friend," said Sarah.

"I see. In the same way you helped your friend who drowned in the river?"

Sarah made herself stay calm.

"No," she said. "That was different. That was my friend who was killed."

"Really?"

"But my colleague and I, who are looking at this, think it is possible that the police may be mistaken in regarding this as an accident. And if that's the case, I'm surprised you wouldn't be interested in hearing more."

Sarah watched Susan consider this. She took a glass of water from the table, sipped, and put it back down.

Taking time to think…

"I assume this 'friend' you mention, is Dominic, yes?"

"Sorry — I really can't say who it is."

This, Sarah thought, *is fun.*

"You know he's just using you, don't you? Taking advantage of your naiveté to slander me and increase his chances of getting the whole estate — all at the same time."

"I have not said who I am helping here, Ms Hamblyn."

"Well, you can't be working for Terry. That drunken little shit couldn't hire someone to cut his hair let alone finesse an inheritance."

Sarah remained silent.

"So it must be someone else in the village," Ms Hamblyn continued. "God, I hate Cherringham sometimes. People interfering, not minding their own business. No wonder I work here in Oxford."

"I know the feeling," said Sarah, trying hard to bring the other woman onside. "It was… circumstance… took me there from London."

"Oh, yes. I remember now — you got dumped, didn't you? High-flyer gets left with the kids?"

"Something like that," said Sarah levelly, refusing to be angered.

"Bad luck."

"No — bad choice of husband," said Sarah.

"Ha!" said Ms Hamblyn. "Is there ever a good choice of husband? God!"

Sarah couldn't help but laugh. And Susan Hamblyn laughed with her. Sarah hoped that the shared laughter might transform her.

So Susan Hamblyn had been unlucky in love? Maybe that's what had made her so tough, so brittle, so unforgiving on the surface.

Sarah decided to try another tack.

"Please don't think I'm interfering, Ms Hamblyn. The person who asked me to get involved in this was truly fond of your father and would hate to think his death was deliberate. But anything you can tell me that might help us put an end to such thoughts would be welcome."

Susan Hamblyn hesitated as if weighing up the pluses and minuses, like columns of numbers. She took a breath.

"All right. But to be honest, there's very little I can tell you. I put a lot of time into looking after my father. I run his accounts, look after the paperwork — I got him a carer — Hope Brown. If there was foul play — then it certainly wasn't from me. To be honest, I expect when the will is read that I shall be the single beneficiary. I know that my father appreciated my loyalty and hard work."

"And what about your brothers?"

"By all means speak to them. Terry's a total loser, as you saw at the funeral. You were there, weren't you?"

"Yes."

"I thought I recognized you. Anyway, Terry — he used to go round to the Manor and get dad drunk then pinch anything he could find and sell it."

"Steal from his own father?"

"All the time. Nice, hmm? That was until Dad eventually wised up and took his key and told him to stay away."

"What about Dominic?"

"That fool? The woman he married has him wrapped round her little finger. Vanessa Coole. I ask you — can that be her real name? Awful woman. A real viper. Now if you're looking for an arsonist, I wouldn't trust her as far as I could throw her. She got Dominic to install one of their ridiculous kitchens — all but forced me to pay for it out of Dad's accounts on the basis the old one was a fire hazard. Dad hated it. Anyway, I know for a fact they think they'll inherit. Idiots."

"Why idiots?"

"You've seen the place, haven't you? It's falling down. It'll cost a small fortune to repair. More than the place is worth. And that's why I can assure you nobody set fire to Mogdon Manor on purpose Ms Edwards: it wasn't even worth burning."

"I see."

Sarah watched as the other woman sat back and checked her watch. This interview was nearly over.

"Just one more question, Ms Hamblyn. A rather difficult one, I hope you don't mind."

"Go ahead."

"Apparently your father was found at the top of the house in the attic room. A locked room nobody ever visited. I wonder if you have any idea what he might have been doing there?"

Sarah wasn't prepared for the effect her question had on the other woman. She watched as Susan Hamblyn seemed almost to deflate, to sink into the deep leather of the sofa.

"No. That's something I don't understand. He'd have to climb the stairs. How could he? We put the stair lift in because he could hardly manage the main stairs, let alone…"

"So, why do you think he went up there?"

"I've no idea. That room was… For some reason it was very important to him. Growing up, after mother died, we sometimes saw him disappear up those stairs for hours. Lock the door behind him. Not come out till late."

"But you never went in yourself?"

"Oh no. Not allowed. Pain of death, he used to say — and I used to think he meant it."

"So what do you think he did up there?"

Susan Hamblyn stared into the distance — as if she was

staring straight into the past, thought Sarah.

"We never knew. Though one day — when I was just a girl — I listened outside the door on the landing and I heard… I swear… singing. He was singing to himself. Very quietly. Such a sad song."

"What was the song — do you remember?"

"Well, that was the really odd thing. He always said that the only other language he could speak was French. But this song — it was in a language I'd never heard. And he knew every word."

8.

A HAPPY COUPLE

STANDING OUTSIDE THE country-chic double frontage of Coole Designs, Jack suddenly regretted not swapping assignments with Sarah. A trip to Oxford, lunch in one of those ancient pubs, maybe even take in a movie …

Instead here he was in the rain, contemplating what line he was going to take in an investigation which — on the surface — was based on little more than a body being found in the wrong place.

Fortunately, he didn't have to make the decision — it was made for him.

"The Rangemeister 5," said a woman's voice next to him. "You're not the only one who's stood out here admiring it. Wanting it — am I right?"

Jack turned. The woman who'd addressed him was standing close — slightly closer than the situation required. Medium height, brunette, heavily made-up, tanned and with collagen-pumped lips. And the very slightest of hints that she'd had a glass of wine with her lunch.

"Well, to be honest, it's not really for me."

The woman squealed with delight.

"You're American!"

"I am."

"I *love* Americans!"

"Well... Isn't it my lucky day?"

"Then — you're right. Far too flashy. I imagine you're more a Shaker style, wood-burning kind of man — am I right?"

"I can't say I've ever thought about myself in terms of ovens, but now that you mention it..."

She slid her arm though his without invitation.

"Come in out of this rain and let's get ourselves a *cawfee* brewing on the stove!"

Jack forced himself to smile at her Americanese, though inside he felt just dread at the thought of where this meeting would go.

The woman opened the door to the store and ushered him inside.

"I'm Vanessa Coole by the way."

"Ah. Coole as in Coole Solutions?"

"The very same!"

"And there I was thinking it was Coole like in Shoppe — you know, with the 'e' on the end like in the Goode Olde Days?"

"Oh, that's perfect!" said Vanessa, clapping her hands." You *are* clever! How wonderfully funny!"

"Isn't it just?" said Jack, keeping a straight face.

"Now you wait here and I'll get the coffee going," said Vanessa, heading to a small kitchen at the back of the showroom.

Jack scanned the shop.

One side was all gleaming cookers and ranges — high-end stuff. He turned over a price list — even the cheapest appliance was in the low thousands. Cherringham might have its poorer areas, like any village, but there was clearly no shortage of locals who were prepared to pay the price of his car for a cooker.

He walked over to the other half of the shop.

Same expensive look and price tags — but this was all marble and granite and glass worktops, and staggeringly pricey wood floors. At a desk in the corner sat a well-built, casually dressed man, leaning back, his hands behind his head, watching.

"Can't beat wood, eh?"

"For certain things, it's unbeatable," said Jack, nodding to him.

The man got up, came over and gently touched Jack on the upper arm.

"Dominic Hamblyn. My wife looking after you okay?" he said.

"Oh yes," said Jack. "I think she's even making me a coffee."

"You're honoured," said Dominic, laughing. "She never makes me one!"

Jack forced a laugh too.

"So what are you after?" said Dominic, stepping back like a salesman in an Istanbul carpet shop. "Oak? Maple? Hi-tech — or maybe organic? We're not the cheapest in the Cotswolds and we never will be. But we'll always be the absolute best."

"I'm sure you are, Mr Hamblyn," said Jack carefully. "But in truth, I'm not after a new floor — beautiful as your floors are."

"He's after a wood-burner, darling, I'm sure of it," said Vanessa, joining them and to Jack's eyes making rather too obvious a show of an affectionate arm around her husband's waist.

"I'm afraid you're both wrong," said Jack, knowing that he wasn't going to be able to sustain this jolly banter any longer.

He noticed both Dominic and Vanessa cool noticeably and wondered what it was they both clearly feared: the tax man? Creditors? The police, even?

For as soon as Jack revealed that he wasn't a customer, they'd both gone instantly into defensive body language. Vanessa withdrew her arm from her husband's waist; Dominic stepped back and folded his arms. They were clearly waiting for him to explain.

"I'm looking at circumstances around the death of your father, Mr Hamblyn, and I'd like to ask you some questions if I may."

"Who the hell are you?" he said, staring at him coldly.

"My name's Jack Brennan. I'm helping someone who knew Victor Hamblyn and asked me to clarify one or two irregularities around what happened."

"Irregularities?" said Vanessa. "What does that mean?"

The banter was definitely gone.

Jack knew he was going to have to manage these two very carefully.

"I realize this is unexpected…"

"Too bloody right it is!" said Dominic.

"I would have made an appointment, but to be honest I was passing and felt we could just chat informally."

"Chat?" said Dominic. "You want me to 'chat' about Dad's death to you, a complete stranger?"

"Victor's death was a terrible shock, Mr Brennan," Vanessa interrupted smoothly.

"Exactly," said Dominic. "And we've still not got over it. You can't just come in here and do this to us!"

"I'm sorry — both of you," said Jack calmly. "But the person I'm… working for… has expressed surprise not only about the source of the fire but also about where your father was found on the night it happened."

"It's bloody Susan, isn't it?" said Vanessa.

"I really can't tell you," said Jack.

"That bitch, she just won't let go," she continued. "Everything we tried to do for poor Victor — the lovely kitchen, which we did at cost by the way — the wiring, the lights, all that time Dominic spent, not a word of thanks, always arguing, turning Victor against us, it was just so..."

She turned away sobbing. Jack frowned — *was this for real?*

He watched as Dominic turned with her, arms around her to comfort.

"I'm sorry, Mrs Hamblyn — I really didn't mean to upset you."

Dominic turned from his wife, his tanned face now reddened, and faced Jack.

"Well, you bloody did," he said. "And just for the record, we did a lot of work on the Manor beyond the kitchen, Mr Brennan. The place was a death-trap, but my electrician and I, we spent time and money re-wiring just to prevent an accident like that happening."

Dominic looked at Vanessa as if checking that she was okay with him talking like this.

"Maybe if my damned sister hadn't been so obstructive, we would have finished the job and my father would be alive now. But she knew she wasn't going to share in the inheritance — and she didn't want us to."

The next words practically sputtered form Dominic's mouth.

"If anyone's to blame for his death, it's Susan. And that's the end of the matter. You've upset Vanessa — and you've upset me too. So I think it's time you left — don't you?"

"Just one last question," asked Jack, going for broke. "What do you think your father was doing in the attic?"

"How the *hell* would I know?" said Dominic. "He wasn't all there at the end. Who knows what was going on inside that mind of his? You've heard the expression a closed book — well, that was my dad, Mr Brennan. Closed, and never opened."

Should he try one more question?

Why not?

"And what about your brother, Terry?" said Jack. "Do you think he might be able to help?"

"Get the hell out of here now," said Dominic. "Before I call the police."

And Jack left, thinking there was a first time for everything — and that was the first time in his life he'd left with that particular warning being issued…

9.

GETTING NOWHERE

SARAH HAD CALLED to invite Jack to join her for lunch at her parents' but she was running late and Jack probably had them all to himself.

He'll manage, she thought.

When she pulled up to the house, Jack's Sprite sat outside in the autumn sun. She parked and raced up the steps.

Her breathless 'hello' was lost amid the sound of an opera quite literally blasting the house.

She followed the music to the sunny sitting room that overlooked the garden. Jack sat in her father's favourite wing-back chair, one arm raised conducting an invisible orchestra, while her Dad commandeered the stereo, all hands on deck should even more volume be needed.

"Er, hi?" she said competing with the music.

Her dad was quick to hit the volume and the opera lowered to the level of lift music.

"Sarah," her dad said. "I was just…"

Jack turned, big smile on his face.

"Jack, so sorry I'm late. Chloe called from school, had some questions."

His grin broadened. "No worries. Michael was sharing one of the best with me."

"'Madama Butterfly' sung by Callas, 'Un bel di'," her dad said as if announcing that he had bagged a prize specimen on a big game hunt.

Sarah turned to Jack. "I forgot that you liked opera."

Jack gave her dad a small nod. "Probably don't know as much about it as your father."

"Oh, I'm just a buff."

"But Katherine got me into it. Took a bit of training, but I learned to love it."

His eyes seemed to drift a bit at the mention of his dead wife. But then he recovered.

He turned to her dad again. "It was beautiful. Thank you."

"Any time, Jack. Just pop on over, and I'll be glad to sip a brandy and listen with you."

"I may just take you up on that."

Sarah's father hurried towards her, rubbing his hands together. "So, Mum's fixing some sandwiches, and tea. We'll have it in here, okay?"

Sarah nodded. "I don't have a lot of time. Big project that I must get out today."

"Right." Her father raised a finger. "I'll go see how things are coming along."

Sarah turned to her partner in crime.

And they brought each other up to date on their first steps in what — so far — wasn't a very fruitful investigation.

Jack nodded. "Right, same with Dominic. Not the best son in the world — and that wife! But could they actually plan a fire, to kill the old man?"

"I know," Sarah said. "Susan Hamblyn is a cool piece of work. And mind you, she too believes that she will inherit it all."

"And Terry? Ever get a show called 'The Three Stooges' over here?"

Sarah grinned at that. "Bit before my time! But I think it was too violent for our telly."

Jack nodded. "That's for sure. Kids loved it."

"So, what next?"

"I have a few ideas…" Jack started but paused when Michael came in with a tray, cups and the family's best teapot decorated with Renaissance figures bowing and curtseying.

"Tea first. Sandwiches along presently. Come on, Sarah sit yourself down."

Sarah pulled a chair closer to the small bistro table that was improbably scheduled to hold the tea and the sandwiches.

She poured a cup for Jack, her dad, then one for herself, the steam swirling up among the dust motes in the air, lit by the low autumn sun.

"So — I hear you two are at it again, hmm? Regular private detective agency?"

Sarah wasn't sure how her parents felt about 'investigating' — or her friendship with the American detective.

Her dad was always a cautious one.

Jack took the query.

"Just helping a friend of Sarah's."

"Hope Brown," Sarah added.

Her dad nodded.

"Seems like it might be suspicious. But maybe not. Won't hurt to look around, ask some questions."

She noticed how when Jack spoke about what they were doing, his voice changed. She felt the authority that he must have carried as detective back in Manhattan.

And — he could turn it on or off with ease.

"I see. Hope is such a good carer. She's helped a lot of

people in the village. I guess if she's concerned then…"

Jack took a sip and then: "Michael, did you know the man at all?"

"Victor? Well, not really. Past few years he's been a recluse, as you know. Didn't get out."

Jack nodded.

"But," her dad put down his tea cup, "I have to tell you, a few years back, I did visit Victor. I knew he had been in the diplomatic service, worked for the government, like me. Didn't think he got many visits, not even from those awful children of his …"

Helen came in with a second tray, filled with sandwiches and small plates that matched the tea service.

"There you are, Sarah," she said.

Sarah gave her mother a smile and tried to make space for the sandwich platter, the plates, the napkins.

"Perhaps we should have this in the dining room," her mother said.

But Jack and Michael helped make space, pushing the teacups one way or the other, and amazingly the tray and its tower of sandwiches made a safe landing.

"There. Enough room, I think."

Helen smiled. "There's a lovely tuna with cucumber, bit of mutton and redcurrant jelly on a whole grain bread, and, of course, egg mayo."

Sarah saw Jack smile at that. "Egg mayo. One of my faves, or as we say 'egg salad'."

That made Sarah's mum laugh. "Never understood that; it's not anything at all like a salad. Well, enjoy."

And sitting around the small table, each of them grabbed a triangular quarter of sandwich of their choice and started eating.

Sarah's dad wiped his mouth with his napkin. "As I was saying. I decided to visit the old man…"

Resuming his story brought a look from his wife. "We're not talking about Victor Hamblyn, are we? Poor soul. And you two — playing detectives."

"Well, Jack *is* a detective," Sarah said.

"Was," Jack added. Then, with perfect timing, "But it is a bit like learning to ride a bike. You never forget." He flashed Helen a smile before turning back to Michael. "You were saying?"

"I like to look in on others who have left the service whether military or the government. Makes a man feel good. And Victor seemed perfectly happy to see me."

Jack shot Sarah a glance as if saying… *you never know where a bit of valuable information can pop up.*

"He was a tad more mobile then. Didn't require as much care, to be sure. And I don't think he had that stair lift thing. Anyway, I had a nice visit with him, reassuring him that we were close should he need anything."

"Because it's doubtful his kids ever said anything like that to him!" Helen added. Sarah knew that this, from her mother who didn't often judge people, must mean that she really didn't like Victor's children.

"I get the impression that they weren't a very close family," said Sarah, pouring herself another cup of tea.

"Yes, I think that's right. And Victor's wife died when the children were still young," said Helen.

"So Victor brought them up on his own?" said Sarah.

"In a fashion, yes," said Helen.

"Can't have been easy," said Jack. "But, Michael — I wonder — did he ever talk about India?"

"I know he served out there as a young man. Difficult post,

right after the war, that country about to fall into turmoil. End of an empire, and all that. And his house was filled with things from there, that big elephant statue—"

"Ganesh," Sarah's mum added.

"And all sorts of Indian stuff. But when I brought up his years there, he simply *clammed up.*"

"Interesting," Jack said. "The conversation just stopped?"

"Exactly. As if the memory was too painful, or something had happened that he didn't want to remember, or certainly didn't want to talk about. I mentioned him at the Rotary club, and old Praveer took me to one side, said that for many who lived through Partition it was best to leave it in the past."

"Partition?" said Sarah.

"When India got her independence in '47. There was a lot of violence. It was a terrible time by all accounts."

"You think perhaps Victor was caught up in that?" said Jack.

Sarah saw her father's face furrow.

"He was certainly serving out there," he said. "Anyway — whatever it was, it was his secret and he wasn't sharing it with me."

The room fell silent.

"All ready for cake?"

Sarah turned to her mum and placed her hand on her mother's arthritic fingers.

They're getting on, she thought. *Need to remember that.*

"I would love a piece, Mum. Really. But I must get back to the office."

"More deadlines, darling?"

"Jack?" her dad said.

"I too would love some but," he patted what was really a very small belly, "think I'd best save dessert for next time."

Sarah's mum gave her hand a squeeze back before looking

from Jack to Sarah.

"You will be careful, yes? The two of you?"

"Mum, there's no…"

But Jack, his voice solid, grounded gave the perfect answer.

"We will indeed."

And that voice, the assuredness, made her mum smile.

"Then let me clear this away and you two can get going."

OUTSIDE THE HOUSE, Jack stopped by his car.

"I like those two."

Sarah nodded. Though it wasn't always perfect, she was one of the lucky ones who actually got on with her parents. And somehow, it seemed important that Jack liked them as well.

"I'm glad," she said. "Interesting story from my Dad, eh?"

Jack nodded. "And unexpected. Some old secret. Does it have anything to do with what happened?" He gave a shrug.

"What next?" Sarah said.

"Up for a bit more digging?"

Sarah nodded.

"Okay," said Jack. "Good. I'm going to visit the village's real estate offices."

"Estate agents."

"Right. Pretend that I'm growing tired of the barge, and maybe hinting I have piles of cash for a property. Get some idea of what that manor house might be worth. If it was burned by one of Victor's children, they would have found out if it had value."

"Good. I'm a bit swamped this afternoon, but is there something you had in mind for me?"

"If you have time, I was thinking a visit to the local electrician's might be worthwhile. If they had fires there previously, some wiring repairs must have been done. And we know Dominic did some."

"I know just who to see," she said. "Been a fixture in the village for decades. I'll try and pop in when I get my layouts sent out."

"Great. And we can touch base this evening?"

"Absolutely."

Another nod, and Jack opened the door to the Sprite. But Sarah put out a hand to his arm to stop him.

"And Jack — thanks for reassuring my mum. She needed to hear that. From you."

"About being careful?"

"Yes."

"Easy to say, Sarah, since I meant it."

A small breeze kicked up, sending orange leaves scurrying under the small sports car.

"Getting chilly," Jack said. He angled his big frame into the too-small driver's bucket seat. "Going to have to put the top up soon."

"The village in winter? You'll love it."

"I bet I will."

And then Jack started the engine and Sarah walked back to her Rav 4.

Autumn was definitely in the air, and winter — waiting in the wings.

10.

PROPERTY VALUES

JACK HAD SPOTTED more than a couple of estate agents in the village. Sales and rentals must be good, based on all the pictures of pricey properties covering their front windows.

Made sense — nice part of the world, he thought.

Though — in some ways — not that different from Manhattan. People still did bad things to each other, people still had their secrets, and there was still a need for people like Jack to ask difficult questions.

He pulled the collar of his jacket up, the chilly wind finding its way through the narrow streets.

About to enter one agent's office, he took a breath and hoped he looked like a well-off client in search of a big property.

Two down, and this last one to go.

Both conversations useful but tricky to end. The important thing was that both agents confirmed what he suspected — Mogdon Manor may not be worth all that much with the massive amount of repairs and restoration it needed. Would take a small fortune just to get it up to code, let alone desirable.

But the property, the grounds?

Easily worth millions.

One could bulldoze the Manor, and still walk away with a ton of cash.

He debated skipping the last of estate agents, Cauldwell & Co, at the far end of the town, near the car park. Looked smaller than the others, maybe dealing with less glitzy properties.

But as he often reminded himself, you never knew where something useful would pop up.

So he went in, his act as prosperous owner-to be now well honed.

A man at a large wooden desk raised his head from the *Daily Telegraph* and immediately flashed Jack a broad grin.

Like estate agents anywhere, they do love when a fresh body walks into their place, he thought.

"Ah, hello! Can I be of assistance to you?"

The man had walked out from behind the desk and grabbed Jack's hand and vigorously pumped it.

"Cecil Cauldwell of Cauldwell & Company."

"Jack Brennan."

"And are we looking for something?"

"As a matter of fact…"

"An *American!*" The agent interrupted. "Can tell that accent anywhere. Looking for a summer rental perhaps, or maybe…"

"Actually — thinking I might be looking for a place to purchase."

Could Cecil's smile get any broader? Jack didn't think so.

"Fan-tastic! Well, you have come at the right time. Things get low sales-wise just as soon as summer fades. So perfect timing for a good buy! Please…" he gestured to a leather chair facing his desk.

Jack began thinking if there was any way to shorten his charade and still get any information from the proprietor.

Cecil had whipped out a yellow pad, grabbed a pen, and —

eyes bright — looked ready to transcribe whatever Jack might say.

"Now, regarding the potential property, it would help me if I knew your price range, and what particulars would be important to you."

Jack nodded. "My price is pretty flexible."

Cecil made a broad 'O' with his lips. Perhaps interpreting 'flexibility' to mean equal unlimited resources.

"Then, you are looking for something in the village, or maybe a country house of some kind? Perhaps with a bit of property?"

Jack scratched his head.

"Not sure. Been living on a river barge so not too sure what I'd want."

The words 'river barge' seem to have a deflating effect. Perhaps Cecil thought that someone living on a barge couldn't possibly be looking at high-end properties. He'd be right about that.

"I did see that old Manor House. Looked damaged, needing work. Too big maybe, but I don't know — interesting."

Cecil's smile faded even further. "Mogdon Manor, yes, quite in need of repair. And the property has been totally let go."

"Would you say the house is worth much?"

Cecil laughed. "That old house? Maybe if you favour claptrap and *fin de siècle* that's truly *fin.*"

"And the grounds?"

"Different story, Mr Brennan. The grounds have not been maintained, but that location, absolutely *prime*. You wouldn't be looking to develop, would you? Maybe some flats or…"

"Who knows. It did catch my eye."

Jack had the confirmation he needed. Property worth a lot, house *nada*. But he asked a last question anyway.

"So the place itself, worth nothing?"

But Cecil raised a hand.

"Hang on. As *is*, probably not. It is in need of massive repairs. But the potential? Someone had it surveyed recently for possible flats. As I said — a lot of potential!"

Jack stopped.

"Surveyed? Who did that?"

Cecil froze, then recoiled to the back of his seat, as if aware that what was going on here was more than chit-chat about the local real estate scene.

"I'm afraid I can't tell you that. Confidential. I was just…"

Jack leaned forward to close the distance.

"You mean, Cecil… that someone had the property surveyed, plans drawn up all in secret? It must be a secret since you're not telling me."

At that Cecil Cauldwell of Cauldwell & Co. stood up.

"I think it's time you left Mr Brennan." He rolled his eyes. "If that's even your name."

"Oh it is." Jack grinned. "You can check."

He started for the door out.

"Hope you don't mind if I pass that information along, do you. Maybe the police? All so interesting."

Cecil stood silent, frozen.

And as Jack walked back to his car, again he thought… *NYC, Cherringham, everyone, everywhere with their secrets.*

Jack sat in his car, the engine rumbling. He'd call Sarah later, after her dinner with the kids.

Now, time for the barge, a medium-rare steak and a martini.

There's something here, he thought.

And that always gave him an appetite.

11.

A MATTER OF ELECTRICITY

SARAH GOT TO her car; her client's files all cleaned up and sent. Time to dash and pick up Chloe.

Except, she realized — amazed — that she was early. Chloe's dance group up at the school didn't finish for another half hour.

There was just time for a coffee and maybe — that rare thing these days — twenty minutes of 'me' time. She locked the car and walked across the village square towards Huffington's, already feeling cheerier.

But Huffington's was closed. She remembered — as the autumn nights drew in, and the summer visitors dried up, they shut on the dot of five.

Half an hour — time to visit Robinson's Electric? Would it still be open?

Then she noticed the old-fashioned neon sign announcing 'electrician' still on.

Not surprising, she thought — the old place couldn't afford to close early with all the discount stores and online competition.

Old Josh Robinson somehow made a living selling toasters

and bedside lights and fuses — though Sarah was sure people only shopped there now out of loyalty.

And why not — Josh was a lovely man, always helpful, always had the time of day.

But Josh also had two sons who were qualified electricians — and who between them did most of the electrical work in the village. Where better to ask for the low-down on electrical work at Mogdon Manor?

The doorbell pinged as she went in. Mr Robinson sat on a stool behind the counter — as he had, she felt, since she was a little girl.

"Ah, Sarah," he said. "How are you, my dear?"

"All the better for seeing you, Mr Robinson," and seeing his jovial face, Sarah suddenly realized she meant it.

"Come for more of those funny long-life eco spots have you? Well, you're in luck: I ordered an extra couple for you back in the spring — thought you'd be needing them!"

"You must be psychic," she said, racking her brains for any other business she could put his way. "I need a new security light as well — for the front door."

After Mr Robinson had spent ten minutes talking through the various options on security light installation, and had rung up the sale on his old-fashioned till, Sarah felt it was time to mention Victor's funeral.

"Ah, yes," said Mr Robinson. "Old Mr Hamblyn. My father always had time for him — though I have to say when I was a lad we always thought he was a miserable beggar. Always yelling at us to get off his land."

"They say it was an electrical fire," said Sarah innocently.

"Yes. Doesn't surprise me," he replied. "My lads have been in and out of the place this year replacing bits of wiring, but they said it was a waste of time doing it piecemeal — the whole system needed ripping out and starting again."

"They must have been upset when they heard about the fire," said Sarah.

"Oh, they were," said Mr Robinson.

He leaned across the counter towards her and lowered his voice.

"Though — between you and me — they reckon Mr Hamblyn was hard done by."

"Oh yes?" said Sarah, leaning in a little herself.

"Well, those kids of his. They could have taken better care. Instead… well, I shouldn't…"

"What?"

"Like they couldn't wait for him to pass away. It was disgraceful."

Sarah nodded.

"And what do you think about this latest fire?" she said. "Another case of bad wiring?"

Josh looked around as if uncomfortable with what he was about to share.

"My son Todd. They asked him to take a look at it. Part of their investigation, you know."

"Yes."

"So he did. Now, most electrical fires just spark a bit behind the walls. Even those old places designed to keep any frayed wires away from the wood."

"But this was different?"

Josh nodded. "Todd said that there was nothing in the library to overload the wiring. Yet something triggered a fire there, in a room full of books! He said it didn't make sense at all."

"It wasn't like the other fires at the manor, you mean?"

Josh stared right at her, his suspicion something she could

feel.

"Exactly. He told the fire chief. Not sure if they thought it meant anything, whole place such an electrical mess. And truth be known, it could be nothing."

Sarah nodded. This was definitely something to tell Jack.

But then an old grandfather clock in the corner of the shop started to chime.

Sarah turned to it.

"I've always loved that clock," she said smiling.

"Yes, keeps on — just as I do."

"And I must run. Pick up my daughter."

The old man reached out and took Sarah's hand. "So good to see you again, Sarah."

"You too."

And with a last smile, Sarah left the shop and headed back to her car.

12.

NIGHT IN CHERRINGHAM

"SO, NO STARS for mum's dinner tonight?"

Sarah watched as her two children wolfed down the chicken fricassee that she had whipped up. Bit of lemon, fresh tarragon, portabello mushrooms, brown rice. Fresh, tasty and, with hungry kids, not destined to last long on the plate.

Daniel paused in mid-forkful to say, "It's good, Mum."

Chloe quickly agreed. "Yup, really good."

Might as well have been a meal from the frozen aisle at Sainsbury's.

"Thanks," she said. "And any school updates?"

Sarah feared that she had already entered that teen realm where kids shared information only under the pain of torture or losing Wi-Fi privileges.

"Daniel, how's the play going?"

"It's a musical, you know," he said. "Weird. 'Macbeth'."

"Isn't that a play?"

"Not this version," Daniel said. "Even the weird sisters…"

"The witches?"

"Yeah, even they sing too. But it's fun,"

"Are you one of the weird sisters?" Chloe said to him. But

her tease was quickly followed by a smile.

We've been through a lot, she thought.

Seems like everyone is trying to be as nice as they can be.

"Well, we'll all be there on opening night."

Daniel nodded. "There's some great battle scenes, with swords and stuff."

"Mum, I'm done."

"Right, Chloe. You can head off to do your homework. I'll clear."

She watched Daniel scoop up the last bit of thick tarragon sauce.

So, a hit, she thought. And pretty easy to do.

"Me too," Daniel said.

"Okay, rinse, dump the plates in the machine, and…"

Then her mobile, recharging at a socket near the stove, rang.

She heard Jack on the phone, but also a sound of something brushing against the phone.

Wind, she guessed. Maybe he was outside on the deck of his barge.

She walked out to the living room, far away enough that her kids wouldn't hear.

"I spoke to the electrician," she said.

She updated Jack on Josh's thoughts on the fire. How his son Todd said it was different from the others, with no evidence in the library to say that something triggered an overload, bad wiring or not.

"Hmm," Jack said. "And I played rich American with your estate agents today."

"You deserve a medal for running that gauntlet."

"They can be persistent, can't they? But I learned something very interesting."

"Do tell."

"Someone — unnamed — had plans drawn up showing how the manor house could be renovated and divided into upscale flats."

"Really?"

"Think the agent — Cecil Cauldwell…"

"Oh. That one. You *do* deserve a medal."

"… Think maybe he thought I was looking for something similar."

"All done, Mum!" Chloe shouted from the kitchen.

Sarah smiled. "Thanks Chlo!" she called out.

Then back to Jack. "Did Cecil reveal who had this done?"

"No. I'm afraid that's when he went all quiet and wanted me to leave his establishment *asap*."

"But we can guess who."

"Three guesses at least. But which one? Susan, Dominic… Terry?"

"Doubt the latter."

"I imagine you are right there. Still — I think we should pay Terry a visit at his trailer."

"Caravan."

"Right. After all, he was looking for something in the house when Hope gave me the tour."

"Tomorrow morning?"

"Perfect. I'll pick you up. And no worries… I put the top up. I'm all set for my English fall."

"Good. Say half-ten?"

"Right."

Then Jack was quiet for a moment and Sarah, beginning to understand how Jack worked, guessed there was something he wasn't saying.

"And tonight, Jack, just some telly, a walk for Brady?"

He cleared his throat.

"Well, I had an idea. If Terry was rummaging around the place looking for something, something of value, then maybe I should try to find it first."

"Going to call Hope? To let you in again?"

"No. If I do find something, and if we want to use it, then best she knows nothing about it. Make sense?"

"Yes. Okay, I can meet you there, but not till…"

"I think no again. Just let me noodle around, on my own. If I do get spotted, you won't have to run down to the police station with me, yes?"

"Okay. But be careful."

Sarah just realized she had echoed the words her mother said.

"Always. But there is one thing you can do. This evening, or maybe in the morning."

"Go on."

Standing by her front door, Sarah again realized how much she enjoyed all this. It was, amid the quiet of her business and village life, *exciting*.

Funny how things work out, she thought.

"Maybe you can make a few calls, see if you can find out what firm did the plans, and who booked them."

"Tough one that." Then she had an idea. "Wait, I could use Grace in the office. She's in touch with quite a lot of the companies, checking on their web and printing needs. And any architectural firm will have their own P.A.s. A little friendly chit-chat, and maybe she could find out who did the plans."

"And who commissioned them? Great."

Again, that sound, and Sarah thought that Jack was probably near the manor house, sitting in his sports car, lights and engine, off.

Waiting for night, about to go in.

And that too was exciting.

Then: "See you in the morning Sarah. Half-ten," he said.

But his 'half-ten' didn't sound quite right.

"Ten thirty it is," she said laughing. "Good hunting."

"You bet."

And then, the called ended, and Sarah went back to the kitchen and the clean-up.

Though she would much rather have been walking alongside Jack, in the dark, straight into Mogdon Manor.

13.

HIDDEN TREASURE

ALL JACK HAD to do to get the back door of the manor open was put a little weight against it, and the ancient latch popped free of the frame.

He had a flashlight in his back pocket but as he entered what seemed to be a storeroom that led into the kitchen, he kept it off.

Better to let his eyes adjust, and use the flashlight only when he had to.

Never know who might be taking a walk, spot the light… Or the place might even be on the cops' local rounds.

He could still smell the fire, the sodden stench from the hoses that had sprayed the library, ruining the carpet, furniture, and hundreds of volumes of books.

The man's entire life of reading, turned into a soggy mush.

Jack guessed that all that motivated him to do this. Decades of being a detective, and he hated it when someone's life was taken from them, a near personal thing with him.

It always felt good to see a suspect finally found guilty.

At least the dead had that bit of peace.

Though Jack guessed, it was more about his own peace, the

way he wanted the world to be. Crimes solved, people punished.

He shook that thought off — never one to indulge self-reflection for long — and started for the main staircase.

He walked up. The hallway was so black, just the faint light from the two windows at either end of the long corridor. His eyes had adjusted, but still he took very small steps, taking care not to stumble into a chair or lamp positioned to blockade his passage. At one end of the hallway was Victor's bedroom.

Breathing low, moving as silently as he could, he reached the door and slowly turned the handle. The door creaked as it opened.

Inside, the room was stuffy, the smell overpowering, old and familiar. It took him back to the room of his aged father all those years ago. Those weekly ferry rides to Staten Island, the dread of seeing his dad so alone, grumbling, not coping. Dying.

He flicked on the flashlight, fingers wrapped around the lens to mask the beam.

He scanned the room: old heavy furniture, a big iron bed, stripped bare, an old armchair, bookshelves. On the floor more books, and against one wall, some old shelves, most empty, a few with dusty and cobwebbed ceramic pieces.

He even saw an Indian statue, a deity with several arms, hands extended, sitting cross-legged.

But though the statue was missing one of its eight arms, old Victor still hadn't thrown it away, preferring to keep it here in his bedroom.

Jack flicked off the light. Nothing here.

Back into the hallway, he shut the door carefully behind him, trying to make do without the flashlight.

Finally he reached the locked entrance to the attic room.

Only one key, Hope said.

He pulled out a thin bit of rigid wire.

Never stopped me before.

And Jack started working the keyhole, back and forth until he heard a click, a bolt slipping back and if welcoming him the door slowly slid open.

He took a breath.

He didn't get spooked too easily, not with everything he had seen.

But this dark, empty manor house, and the narrow staircase…

Some company right now, he thought, *would be good.*

IN THE ATTIC room again he had no choice but to turn on the small flashlight, wrapping his hand around the lit end to make the beam as narrow as possible.

The place was a puzzle. No boxes. No old furniture. Completely empty. Which in itself was strange, in a house this old and lived-in.

He looked around one more time, letting the light slowly scan the room.

And he noticed something. The room seemed smaller than it should be, based on what this upper floor looked like from outside, and even from the dimensions of the floor below it.

It wasn't uncommon for an attic to narrow, but somehow the size here seemed… *off.*

Which meant…

He let the light play along the angled wood of the roof, the walls, looking for… something.

And then he saw an outline on a wall to the right. To the casual eye, it might look like the grain of the wood, or where one wooden slat joined another. But as Jack went closer, he saw that wasn't the case.

He pressed against it, tapped. A hollow sound answered him back.

And then he realized… the attic contained a *hidden* room.

Amazing, he thought.

But with no door knob, no key, how to get into it?

He started tracing the mystery door's outline with his light.

Jack was beginning to think that he was stumped.

There may be a room on the other side of the wall but he was damned if he knew how to get the flush door to open.

But he was always a big fan of trial and error.

So he began pressing against the nearly invisible outline, listening to what those hard presses did.

And when his hands got to the top, and he pressed hard, he heard something. Some movement or slippage.

And it looked as if a bit of the hidden door bowed out, mere millimetres, but it was *something.*

Could there be latches all around it?

Now he did the same thing, on either side, pressing hard, hearing more sounds, the door popping out a few more millimetres with every push.

Until, kneeling down in the dark attic, he pressed at the very bottom, and the door opened.

Giving up its secrets.

And he stood up, and pulled it wide open.

The room was small, not much larger than a walk-in closet and there were no windows so he could use his flashlight without worry.

And what he saw made him stop.

A small table, covered by rich red material with gold stitching that glistened under his light. On top of it was yet another elephant god but this one was holding something right in its broad lap, as if guarding it, protecting it.

A faded black-and-white photograph of a woman. Dark eyes, long dark hair, dressed in a traditional sari. Her smile was radiant; she was an astounding beauty.

What is this? Jack thought.

A shrine to a lost love?

But then why so secret? Why not keep it downstairs?

The he noticed something on a small shelf suspended on a wall to the right of the table.

An ornate wooden chest with a metal latch, but no lock.

Feeling almost as if he was violating a tomb but compelled to see, Jack tucked his light under an armpit, and picked up the box, opening the lid.

And for a moment he stared, before placing it on the table and leafing through its contents.

Victor Hamblyn's secrets. All *here*.

Behind him all of a sudden, he saw a light hit the attic walls.

He shut the lid, and quickly turned off his flashlight.

He picked up the chest and walked out to the attic room taking care to shut the hidden room's door behind him.

To the window, staying back in the shadows to see some of Cherringham's finest, outside their police car, aiming massive torches up to the attic, and all around the house.

Jack had to move fast.

MOVING AS QUICKLY as he could with no light, his eyes less effective after using the flashlight, Jack ran down the stairs, nearly tripping on the tattered carpet, then around to the back of the house.

He heard fumbling at the front door, and he picked up his speed, feeling like a kid robbing a neighbour. He raced to the big kitchen, bumping into the wooden kitchen table hard, suppressing an 'ouch' before finally reaching the back door and slipping out.

The police hadn't made their way around to the back yet and with the scant light of the stars better than the total darkness inside, Jack raced unseen through the overgrown grounds of Victor's estate, making his way to where he hoped his car remained hidden.

If he didn't get caught, *if* the police didn't take the chest from him and lock him up, he knew he would be up most of the night, looking through the contents of the wooden chest.

Trying to understand.

14.

WHAC-A-MOLE

"ONE MACCHIATO LONG with an extra shot."

Sarah waited patiently as the Huffington's waitress in her trim little outfit, placed Jack's steaming coffee on the pine table in front of him, without spilling a drop.

He looks tired, she thought. *How late was he at Mogdon Manor?*

"And one large Americano, with skinny hot milk on the side."

Sarah smiled her thanks. The girl bobbed politely and left them, in their little table by the window.

"When I was a kid, this place only served instant coffee," said Sarah. "Times change — thank God."

"True," said Jack, pouring the milk into his coffee. "Though the waitress looks like she should be in *Downton Abbey*."

"The Huffington's uniform — a girl must wear it with pride, and I should know."

"More secrets of your teenage past, huh?" said Jack, his eyes twinkling.

"They fired me after a week — couldn't resist eating the cakes."

"I know the feeling," said Jack.

Sarah stirred her macchiato.

"So why the change of plan?" she said. "I've not even been into the office yet."

Jack sipped his coffee. He might look tired but she could see that he was enjoying this moment, she knew him well enough by now to know.

He lifted up an old sports bag onto his lap and slowly unzipped it.

"I had an interesting night. Not entirely legal, but hey I'm one of the good guys so I figure the rules in Olde England are probably flexible."

"Are you about to implicate me in some kind of crime, Mr Brennan?"

"You bet."

"Good. I'd hate to be left out."

"Left out?" said Jack. "You're the key to its success."

And she listened as he told her all about what had happened at the Manor: the attic, the secret room and his unorthodox journey home via a ditch at the back of the property.

"You're lucky the police didn't catch you," she said.

"I might be slower than I used to be — but we cops all work from the same training manual, so I was one step ahead all the way home."

"A long night then?"

"Trouble is — when I hit the sack, I was too tired to sleep."

Though the banter was fun, Sarah couldn't wait any longer.

"So Jack — what have you got?" she said, smiling.

"I thought you'd never ask."

Like a magician he reached into the bag and placed the first item onto the table between them. It was a large wooden box inlaid with ivory figures.

"It's beautiful," said Sarah, picking it up. "Is it Indian?"

She opened it. The inside was red velvet.

"Got to be," said Jack. "Some kind of jewellery box I guess. And it did have jewellery in it."

She saw him take a look around the cafe which was fast filling up.

He leaned in confidentially, carefully drew out a necklace from the bag and held it out. She took it gently from his hands: it was made of beaten gold with black beads threaded onto it. Where it caught the light it glowed.

"It's exquisite," she said, her voice hushed. "Do you think this is what Terry was after?"

"It's certainly valuable — if it's real gold and I'm sure it is," said Jack. "But this is the stuff that's really interesting."

Sarah felt the thrill of real discovery, of unlocking secrets, of finding truths — and here in Huffington's of all places.

She watched as Jack now took out a wad of bank statements held together with an old bulldog clip, and handed them to her. She wiped the dust off and flicked through them.

"Weird," she said. "It's the same transaction over and over again."

"It's a holding account," said Jack. "Two hundred in each month — from Victor's main account I suspect — and two hundred out. Stops about five years ago — and goes back at least thirty."

"But why?"

"It's what you do when you want to hide a payment," said Jack.

Next he produced a bundle of faded letters, held together with a tattered ribbon. He handed it to her, and nodded. Slowly she undid the ribbon, scared that the letters might almost turn to dust.

"There must be a hundred…"

"One hundred and eighty-five, to be precise," said Jack.

She tried to make out the writing — but it wasn't in English, or even in a European language. But though she couldn't read the careful script — she didn't have to ask what was in the letters. She had seen papers bound together like this before.

These were love letters.

From a different time. A different place.

"I did a bit of research when I got back to the boat last night," said Jack. "I think they're written in Hindi."

"I didn't know you could get online, Jack."

"Research — you know like in the old days? With books?" he said. "Those things I have on shelves in my office?"

"Ah, so that's what they are," said Sarah. "So what do the letters say?"

"This is where you come in," he said. "Or rather your dad's friend."

"Praveer?"

"That's the one," said Jack. "We need these translated. Or at least the gist of them. You think he'd be up for that?"

"I don't see why not," said Sarah. "I can get his address from Dad."

"And there's one more thing," said Jack, reaching into his bag and placing on the table some small spools of film. "What do you make of these?"

Sarah picked one up carefully, taking care not to touch the film.

"It's 8mm," she said. "We used to play around with this stuff at art college."

"Pretty old, huh?"

"Definitely. This is what people used before they had Super-8. So certainly pre-sixties."

"You think you can project it somehow?"

"Oh, I can do better than that," said Sarah. "They've got a photography lab up at the school and they do transfers of stuff like this."

"How quickly can you get it done?"

"If I call in a favour — tomorrow, maybe?" said Sarah. "But why the rush?"

"Well here's the thing," said Jack. "Hope called me this morning to say the solicitor is reading Victor's will tomorrow — and her presence has been requested. She'd like us to join her. And I've got a gut feeling we need to solve this little mystery before Victor's miserable kids divide the spoils."

Sarah looked at him — he was back in full-on hard-cop mode.

"Maybe we should talk to the police?"

He shrugged.

"About what?"

And Sarah realized. They hadn't solved anything. They hadn't even uncovered a crime. All they'd done was reveal a more and more complicated series of mysteries. And a family that seemed to hate itself.

"No matter how much we've found," said Jack. "We still don't know a great deal."

Sarah tried to sum up where they'd got to.

"So what do we know? Victor died because he was trying to get to his secret room. But we don't know why he had it hidden and what the significance of what you found in there is. Someone was outside the house when he died — but we still don't know who."

She looked at Jack for confirmation that she was on track here, not missing anything.

"The fire started because of faulty wiring — but in a room he never used. Victor's kids can't wait to inherit and they each think they're going to be the only ones. Oh, and someone's all set to knock the Manor down and make a fortune. But again, we don't know who. Maybe all three of them!"

"See what I mean?" said Jack. "It's a list of suspicions — but nothing we can prove."

"You're right," she said.

"And yet," said Jack, "As the man said — if it smells of fish…"

"It *is* fish. And this smells of fish all right," said Sarah. "Question is — what kind of fish?"

Jack laughed. "Enough fish already!"

She laughed too.

"Time I got to the office," she said. "I want to get Grace onto those plans — see if we can identify our mystery property developer."

"Good," said Jack. "I'm going to hang on to the statements. But you'd better take the rest — see what you can find out."

And placing the film and the letters with the necklace back in the box, he handed it to her.

"I've got to do some running round this morning," he said. "Then I was thinking I'd drop in on young Terry after lunch."

"Want me to come?"

"By all means," said Jack. "Though it might not be pretty."

"On second thoughts — maybe I'll spend a bit of time researching Partition," said Sarah.

"Good call," said Jack, picking up the bill. "Couple of quid tip okay you think?"

Sarah shook her head in mock despair.

"Far too much," she said. "I wish you'd been around when I was waitressing."

And she headed out to the office.

15.

TWO AND TWO

"IN YOU GO, Riley, I'll be back soon."

Jack shooed his Springer Spaniel down into the saloon of the barge, closed the shutters and clicked the padlock.

He climbed down into his little dinghy, powered up the outboard, untied and pushed off from the side of his beloved Grey Goose.

The water was flat calm as he headed downstream, but he could feel a chill in the air and he drew his windcheater collar tight.

Past the weir and under Cherringham Bridge — and five minutes later, there was his destination on the far riverbank: Iron Wharf.

The year before when he'd been looking to buy a boat in the area, he'd been a regular visitor to the old boatyard, scanning the 'for sale' notices, chatting to the locals for information or leads to his dream boat.

Now, as he tied up on the visitors' mooring and clambered up the side of the jetty onto the hard, he realized how at home he felt on the river. In those days he'd been a complete beginner — now it felt the most natural thing in the world to go visiting by boat.

He looked around: the yard was full of old sheds, piles of timber, and boats in all states propped up with great wooden beams. Grass and weeds grew over stacks of rubbish and rusty iron.

Somewhere in here, Terry Hamblyn had chosen to live.

He didn't have to look hard to see where. In a corner of the boatyard stood a ramshackle old trailer, with smoke pumping out of a chimney on the top and heavy metal pumping from an open window.

Bit of a come down from the old manor, thought Jack.

Parked up next to the trailer was a battered old pick-up — and a smart yellow four-by-four with the words 'Monster Madness!!!' stencilled on the side. Jack recognised the brand — they had a big arena the other side of Swindon and advertised 'truck mayhem' aggressively on television.

As he approached, Jack saw the trailer door open and two figures emerge, laughing: one was Terry and the other was a big, balding guy in a leather jacket. Jack hung back and watched as the two did a bit of blokey back-slapping, then shook hands.

The bald guy climbed into the four-by-four, spun it round and with a honk on the horn roared off across the boatyard, kicking gravel behind.

Jack waited till Terry had gone back into the trailer, and then sauntered over. The back of the pick-up was full of rubbish — bits of boat, sacking, a small space heater. Jack examined the heater. The cable was blackened.

Interesting.

A refuse bin overflowing with rubbish sacks, cans and bottles sat by the back door. More out of habit than anything else, Jack peered into the bin and did a double take: some of the wine bottles were old, he was sure. Very old.

He pulled out an empty wine bottle and examined the label. Château Mouton Rothschild 1928.

Jeez — could that be for real?

He sniffed the contents. It was.

My God. That one bottle alone is worth a couple of months' pay.

Jack fished deeper into the bin. There were more bottles of a similar vintage beneath — obviously just thrown into the bin when they were finished, to rest among old curry cartons and cheap cans of lager.

Jack took out a paper handkerchief and wiped his hands, then tossed it into the bin and approached the door of the trailer. Terry Hamblyn had some questions to answer.

"Like I said. Me and dad were best mates," said Terry. "He gave me that wine for Christmas. Because he loved me."

"You know how much that stuff's worth?"

"Sure. Gotta be at least ten quid a bottle. It's real French."

Jack watched Terry, unsure whether to feel pity, anger or simply disgust. They were seated facing each other across Terry's table in the back of the trailer. A thin layer of grease, old food and possibly engine oil coated the surface and Jack was trying hard not to touch anything.

"And you still say you weren't there on the night he died?"

"I was here asleep. Bit of a home boy, me."

Jack looked round the filthy trailer, piled high with unwashed plates, alcohol, magazines and discarded clothes.

"I can see that, Terry. And I really don't want to get you into trouble…"

"I haven't done anything, so you can't."

"But you know, if the police did find out you were there when Victor died, then things might very quickly get… difficult… for you — know what I mean?"

Jack smiled at Terry and was rewarded with a dopey smile back.

"Sure. Appreciate you dropping round to tell me that."

He got up — and Jack saw his cue to leave.

"Any time you need a bit of help in the future — I'll be sure to remember how you came down here to help me," said Terry seriously. "I scratch your back, you scratch mine, know what I mean?"

Jack headed for the door and climbed down the little steps out of the trailer. He could sense Terry standing behind him and turned quickly.

"How's the deal coming along with Monster Trucks?"

Terry didn't stop to blink.

"Pretty good," he said. "Soon as the land's mine we're going to sign the contracts and then…"

Jack could almost see the synapses in Terry's brain connecting.

"And then?"

"Oh, shit," said Terry.

"Thanks for the chat, Terry. See you tomorrow at the reading of the will."

"Eh? What? How come — what's that got to do with you?"

Jack smiled, turned on his heels and walked across the yard to his little boat, feeling that maybe one of these little mysteries was falling into place.

16.

WHAT ARE FRIENDS FOR?

SARAH WAS SUPPOSED to be putting the finishing touches to the Highlands brochure, cropping a wind-turbine out of a near-perfect vista of heather and mountains, but Grace's phone conversation at the other end of the office was just too interesting…

She got up, went to the little kitchen, poured herself a coffee and went over and sat on the corner of Grace's desk.

Grace winked at her and carried on talking into the phone.

"Anyway, I'm going to have to go or the boss'll be back. Saturday? Sure. Me and some of the girls are heading into Oxford. You kidding? It'll be a late one. And I don't mean jim-jams!"

Sarah smiled — nothing changed. Twenty years ago her Saturday nights usually involved having some fun in Oxford — but in those days you had to be back on the last train or else.

But did she want to be Grace's age again? *No thanks!*

"Oh, and Kelly — don't forget, use my private email will you or I'll get into trouble. Sure. Sure — you're a sweetie, see you Saturday!"

Sarah watched as Grace put the phone down — then

rubbed her hands in glee.

"God, I love this Sarah! This is *tons* more fun than doing brochures. Let's be a detective agency!"

Sarah laughed.

"The day I can see a way to make money out of it — you'll be the first to know."

"I'd do it for free!"

"I'm sure you would. But you tell me the moment you feel I'm taking advantage. You will, won't you?"

"Sure," said Grace. "I'm kidding really — but I've had fun this morning."

"So what have you got for me?"

Grace gestured to Sarah to take a seat next to her and she pulled up the notes she'd been making on screen.

"Well, first off you'd be surprised how the old Personal Assistant code of honour works — most people were happy to let me have bits of info as long as they knew it was for a good cause."

"I should be worried by that," said Sarah.

"Don't be — you're one of the good guys."

"God knows what digital information laws you just broke."

"I think you mean 'we', don't you?"

And as Grace laughed, Sarah just had to join in.

"So, starting at the top. The plans for Mogdon Manor which your American heard about were drawn up by Phillips and Co, Chartered Surveyors exactly three months ago."

"Local, huh?"

"And Phillips and Co were instructed by the architects — Dream Designs — about a month before that. And the client who instructed Dream Designs was... hmm, now where did I put that name..."

"Don't do this to me, Grace!"

Grace laughed.

"Ah, here we are," she said. "Susan Hamblyn, Davies Associates, Oxford."

Sarah sat back in her seat.

"Well, isn't that interesting?"

She looked at Grace — but Grace wasn't finished.

"Now that's not the only interesting thing I found," she said, conspiratorially. "When I asked my pal at Phillips about the plans they were working on for Mogdon, guess what she said?"

"Go on — surprise me."

"She said — 'which ones?' — because we've got two. And guess who instructed them about the others?"

Sarah didn't have to think.

"Vanessa Coole, at Coole Solutions?"

Grace played mock disappointment.

"How did you know that?"

"Let's just say I'm beginning to get used to the way the Hamblyn family operates."

"Anyway, they're going to email the plans before they close today," said Grace. "I told them I'd deleted them by mistake and they didn't even ask why I had them in the first place."

Sarah stood up, and noticed for the first time it was beginning to get dark outside.

"Grace, you've done an amazing job. When they come through, print them out for me and leave them on the desk, could you?"

"Sure," said Grace. "Are you heading off?"

"I've got some ancient history to explore with an old friend of my dad's," she said. "But I'll drop by the office in the morning to pick up those plans."

"Did I do well, boss?" said Grace in a joke American accent.

"You sure did, officer," said Sarah. "There'll be a medal in this for you."

"Forget the medal. Just leave me a croissant tomorrow morning and I'll be happy."

JACK WAS WALKING back along the river bank to the 'Grey Goose' in the moonlight when his phone rang.

It was Sarah.

"How are you, Jack?"

"I'm good."

"Sound a little distant."

Jack paused just at the bend in the river where he could see his boat in the distance. The Thames swept silently by just yards away, soft light reflecting from it. Muffled sounds came from the other houseboats lined up along the riverbank.

Across the river in the meadows he could see the outlines of a herd of cattle, still munching silently. Apart from them — he was alone.

"Just walking home."

"I tried you earlier — but you were off the radar."

"Yep," he said. "Went out for dinner."

"Oh. Somewhere nice?"

"Yep. Very."

There was silence on the other end of the phone. An awkward silence, Jack suddenly realized with a smile to himself. He could imagine Sarah wondering if she could ask one more question, just one more… But to his relief, she didn't.

"Good," she said. "Now while you've been discovering that there is such a thing as English cuisine, I've been working on the case."

"Excellent," he said. "I hope you've got some answers."

"You bet."

Jack listened as Sarah went through the information that Grace had gleaned from her pals across the county.

"Kinda chilling," he said, when she'd finished. "And you know what? Susan and Dominic weren't the only ones who had plans for Mogdon."

"Let me guess — young Terry was also planning for his retirement too?"

"You got it. But nothing as simple as apartments. Oh, no. He was going to open Cherringham's first Monster Truck arena. Just what the village needs."

"You have to be kidding."

"Nope."

"What a family," she said, laughing. "But you know what, Jack — I still can't quite see them as killers."

"Killers don't wear a uniform," said Jack. "But listen — what did you find out about the box?"

The chill began to seep through his coat and he started walking again, eager to get back onto the boat.

"I dropped everything off with Praveer," said Sarah. "He promised me he'll read all the letters and get back to me by lunchtime tomorrow."

"They're definitely Hindi, yes?"

"Yes," said Sarah. "But wait till you hear this. The necklace is important. It's symbolic. It's called a Mangalsutra."

"Uh-huh?" said Jack. "What's it a symbol of?"

"Marriage," said Sarah. "In Hindu weddings, the groom gives it to the bride. And it stays with her for life."

Jack stepped onto the deck of boat and stopped to think.

"Well, now I'm really confused," he said. "Unless Victor was a collector — which is quite possible — then I think perhaps he had a real secret."

"A secret that led to his death?" said Sarah.

"Could be."

From inside the boat, Jack could hear Riley scratching, waiting to be let out.

"Sarah — I gotta go."

"Oh one last thing — I dropped the film off at the school and my friend up there said she'd digitize it so I can download it tomorrow morning."

"Sounds good to me," said Jack, unlocking the shutters and stepping back as Riley ran round his legs joyfully. "Hope says they're reading the will on the dot of noon up at the Manor and she'd appreciate both of us being there to support her."

"I'll be there soon as I can," said Sarah. "I just hope the letters give us some answers. We don't even know how the fire started."

"Oh, I do," said Jack. "Tell you tomorrow."

"Jack! Don't do that to me…"

"Ha! I've got a stove to light and a nightcap to enjoy, Sarah — night night!"

And with a smile to himself, Jack called for Riley to come back from the riverbank and headed down into the cabin.

17.

WHERE THERE'S A WILL...

NOW THIS IS classic, Jack thought.

Chairs had been set up in two rows in the manor's large living room, and the Hamblyn family sat at attention, front row, not talking to each other, only sitting stock-still.

Waiting.

Each one of them expecting to be the beneficiary of their father's untimely death.

Inherited money.

Does anything good ever come from it? he thought.

Jack looked at Hope sitting next to him, and she smiled back. They had talked so much at dinner last night — and Jack felt for the first time since Katherine's death that maybe it might be time to, as they say, *get out there.*

Though as much as he liked the good-hearted Hope, he wasn't sure if he was ready. Or ever would be.

The solicitor, Tony Standish, sat at a table that had been dragged to face the grim row of relatives.

He cleared his throat, and looked up.

"Shall we begin?"

Hope shot Jack a look. No Sarah. Maybe a problem with

her work, the translation of the letters?

Either way, Victor's solicitor had no reason to postpone the main event.

Jack leaned into Hope, a whisper: "She'll be here. She wouldn't miss this for anything."

Jack's words summoned a glare and a sneer from Susan Hamblyn.

Keep doing that, lady, and by the time you're my age you will look like one of those baked apple 'heads' the kids make around Halloween.

She had already voiced her opposition to both him and Hope being there, but Standish had overruled her.

Jack wondered whether the solicitor had a few secrets as well.

"Very well." Then a smile from Standish, which did nothing to lighten the mood in this grim room, still reeking of the sodden wood, the burned timbers.

"As you know, I have represented your dear departed father for decades now, ever since my own father passed his practice on to me."

Jack saw Dominic nod, and then lick his lips.

Each one of the potential heirs radiating... *just get the hell on with it.*

"And among other duties, I have been entrusted with the care of your father's will. And there are, in fact, two documents. A will, which my father helped Victor Hamblyn draw up in the autumn of 1952."

He held up a large faded yellow envelope.

"This, the original will, has been sealed since that date. I have no knowledge of its contents. And this..."

Now he brandished a smaller envelope.

"The contents of this were drafted by me, at Victor's instructions, and represent a codicil to the original will. I will read the original first, followed by the codicil."

"Oh, do get *on* with it," Susan Hamblyn muttered.

The comment made Standish sit up straight, as if shocked by the rudeness. Sarah had told Jack that her own family always used Tony for legal matters, and that he was about as ethical and kind as they come.

And now he has to deal with this lot, Jack thought.

"Are there any questions before we begin?"

No one said anything but Jack fired a look at the door. Sarah was indeed missing a great show.

"Very well."

Standish took a long metal letter opener shaped like a rapier, and opened the large envelope containing the 1952 will.

Jack had to admit…this is exciting.

It seemed like all the potential heirs slid a bit forward in their chair, ready to hear every word about their good fortune.

Standish began with what was basic boiler-plate for wills, with references to 'sound body and mind', before he got to the meat of the matter.

Who gets what?

Standish paused, his eyes on the words. This document was, after all, new to him as well. And the length of the pause indicated that in Standish's quick scan, he saw something that stopped him cold.

But with sniff of the musty air in the room, he recovered:

"Therefore, I, Victor Hamblyn, bequeath my entire estate, and all its possessions, to my beautiful wife, Geeta Hamblyn *nee* Anand and all her heirs, to be shared equally."

And with that line, it was as if someone had thrown a packet of firecrackers right into the centre of the living room.

The three not-heirs ran around the desk, trying to yank the aged will out of Standish's hand.

But Standish was quick, tall, and literally held it over his head.

"Please!" he said. "Sit *down*. There must be decorum. This is the reading of the deceased's will!"

Jack wondered whether he might have to stand up to defend the man.

But slowly, like hyenas circling prey at a water hole who then decided to withdraw, Susan, Terry, and Dominic — the latter backed by an equally fierce Vanessa — returned to their seats.

"You've got to read the... the second bit now!" Terry stammered, showing that he had well-fortified himself for the emotional morning to come.

Jack was sure that there were even greater surprises ahead.

He thought about the letters, the 8mm movies, now this woman in the will, Victor's wife — *Geeta?*

How could that be?

But Jack's questions didn't compare to those of the Hamblyn family.

And this ceremony began to seem more like a raucous auction than a sombre reading of a man's last words.

18.

WHAT YOU DON'T KNOW

"THAT DOCUMENT IS pure *rubbish*," Susan Hamblyn said. "Our father was married to *our* mother, Elizabeth. *She's* the wife, we are the heirs. And that is that!"

"Yes, absolutely," Dominic said, joining his sister, all of them now probably thinking that a third of property was better than none.

Standish put the old will down and picked up the other envelope.

"But you see, and this is the odd thing. As your father's solicitor, I should have had a copy of all his important legal documents. And there was one he never provided me."

A pin could drop and the noise would have been deafening.

"Go on," Susan finally snapped.

Standish looked like he didn't know if he could bear to share the bit of information he was about to reveal.

"You see, your father never provided me with his marriage certificate."

The room exploded with "whats?", 'bloody hells" and various forms of "ridiculous" and "damnits".

Standish waited until that storm subsided.

"And I did ask repeatedly."

"Well, I will have my solicitor find that," said Dominic. "Should not be a problem — at all. Local records. A total non-issue."

Standish held up the other, small white envelope.

"Shall I read this now?"

"Yes, please," Dominic said. "I'm sure it will clear up all this nonsense. Geeta, indeed!"

Jack heard a creaking noise behind him, the big door to the manor opening, and in moments, Sarah entered the living room.

The Hamblyn clan barely took notice of her, all eyes locked on the envelope that — Jack guessed — they assumed would save their skins and fortunes.

Sarah shot Jack a smile. She had a laptop in one hand, and a file folder in the other.

No box with the jewel, which was probably a good thing considering the rapaciousness of this crowd.

She sat in a chair next to Hope and patted her friend's hand. Hope whispered to Sarah, getting her up to speed on what was happening here.

Things — Jack felt — were about to get even more interesting...

Again the rapier-like letter opener, slicing a neat incision at the top of the envelope.

Then Standish withdrawing a single sheet of paper.

Of course, he knows full well what's in it, Jack thought.

The solicitor looked up. No smile now.

Jack guessed that the news coming wouldn't be good.

Again, there was more legal language, before getting to the key paragraph.

Another pause. Another dramatic clearing of the throat.

Standish was nearly done, just a few more lines to get through.

"I therefore make, in the presence of my solicitor, Mr Anthony Standish Esquire, one emendation to my previous last will and testament."

The edge of the seats had even more weight applied. Terry Hamblyn now leaned so far forward that he looked ready to catapult to the other side of the room.

"To my dear carer, Hope Brown, I leave the sum of 10,000 pounds in deep appreciation for her kindness and professionalism."

Everyone waited for the next bit.

But there was no next bit.

Vanessa now stood up, taking on the role of spokesperson for them all.

"Well, that measly codicil means absolutely nothing since we know who the old man was married to and it was not Geeta, that's for…"

Sarah stood up, distracting Vanessa from her speech, and walked to the front of the room, her file folder in her hand.

Sarah looked at Jack, who gave her a reassuring smile.

Sarah began quickly since she knew the mayhem that would follow when she was done.

"There was a box. An Indian chest."

"I *knew* it," Terry said, slapping a meaty fist into his palm. "The secret treasure."

"Of a sort."

"Everything in this house, including that box," Susan Hamblyn announced with authority, "will go to the rightful heirs. Us!"

She saw the siblings for once united in their head bobbing.

"I imagine so. It did contain a jewel, a Mangalsutra. A wedding necklace."

Confusion now played on the Hamblyn family's faces.

"And that's not all the box contained. So many letters, sent to his Geeta in India, all returned unread. All love letters."

Sarah paused. Then:

"Oh, and there were some old 8mm films. I had them digitized, and made a disc for each of you. Your father and his beautiful wife... Geeta."

"Geeta?" said Dominic, his face glowing red. "Just who the hell *is* this Geeta woman?"

"She was nobody!" Terry said.

Sarah quickly shook her head. Both Susan and Dominic had their eyes locked on her.

"And there was also a marriage certificate."

She opened the folder and handed a paper to Tony, who immediately began scanning it, then reading.

"June 12, 1946, yes, performed at the British Court House, Bombay. Victor was married to Geeta."

"Impossible!" Susan said.

But Tony looked up at her, then to the others and said, "No. I'm afraid it is perfectly legal, has the raised seal and everything. This marriage certificate proves that his heir and his wife is this woman, Geeta."

"But if that's true..."

Sarah watched Dominic turn from Susan to Terry, all of them seemingly engaged in a competition as to who could look more gob-smacked.

"Then if she was his legal wife, then that means we're all..."

"That's right," Sarah said with a cheery smile. Some days were indeed better than other. "You are all bastards."

And at that Jack had to laugh, as he stood up.

Sarah was glad that Jack came and stood beside her since now the Hamblyn clan had also stood up and started yelling at each other.

"I bet it was *you* who set that idiotic fire," Susan said to Dominic.

"Accusing me to cover for yourself, my dear? Or…"

Dominic spun on his heels towards Terry. "Maybe it was you, the 'brains' of the family, hoping to push things along? After all, you always did barrel on about being dad's favourite."

Amazing, Sarah thought, looking at Tony who clearly wanted to conclude this, and then to Jack whose face showed that it was all too much fun for him.

But as the family took turns accusing each other of setting the fire, of actually killing their father, Jack finally raised his voice.

And that stopped them.

"Hang on, folks. I did some digging around the other night, and I think I can show you who made the fire happen, and how."

A pause, each of them looking guilty.

Could be any one of them, Sarah thought.

"If you will follow me. To the basement."

Jack started for the back door that led to the cellar, and the stairs down, and when one of the Hamblyns did not immediately fall in line, he stopped.

"Coming along, Terry?"

And Sarah saw from the sick expression that Terry might have a clue as to where this would lead.

LATE AFTERNOON SUN still filtered into the narrow windows of the cellar. The room felt chilly, the stone floor uneven.

Jack ducked under low cross beams until he came to a wine cellar, motioning the others towards the wine rack, which looked as though someone had been playing battleships with it — dotted as it was with so many empty slots.

"But where is all the wine? Last time I was down here," Dominic said, "these racks of vintage reds were *full*."

And all Jack had to do was point, and the group turned - to see a pile of empties stood by one wall, looking like glass soldiers mowed down.

"Someone liked to come down here, have a bottle or three," Jack explained. "Maybe bring one back home. But you see…"

Jack walked behind the massive chimney bottom, around to the back, and returned dangling the space heater he'd found in the bin at Terry's caravan.

'Gets quite cold down here at night, after Victor goes to bed. So cold that you need a little space heater to take the chill off. Isn't that right, Terry?"

"I… I just… I mean, he didn't drink any of it so I thought…"

Jack nodded.

"And yes — guess you'd sit… right about here."

A wooden chair with a tattered cushion sat next to the empties. And behind it, an electric wall socket.

And that too was blackened.

"I don't understand," Susan said.

But Jack wasn't about to rush.

He gave them all a smile.

"I imagine the wiring down here is even more ancient than most of the house. And do you know what room is right above here, on the same primitive circuit?"

Everyone looked up to the dark floorboards above them.

Jack could see Sarah, trying to imagine the layout of the ground floor.

But Dominic nodded.

"The library…"

Jack's smile faded.

"Yes. The electrical fire may have started here, an overload… but it triggered the main one up there."

Dominic came and grabbed his brother by the lapel and Terry — though built like a bowling pin — seemed to become an empty bag of air as his brother shook him left and right.

"You killed him! You killed…"

But Jack intervened.

"No. All Terry did here was sample some free if expensive wine. When the heater blew the circuit, I imagine," he turned to Terry "that you grabbed the heater — ran out, panicked?"

Terry nodded.

"I called out to Dad. I thought he'd hear and get out. Then the fire trucks showed up. They'd get him out, I thought."

"So you bolted," Jack said. "Nice."

"Bloody typical," said Susan Hamblyn. "You always did run away, you little…"

And now Jack had to step sideways, to protect Terry from his sister whose hands reached out to grab at his long, greasy hair.

"Please!" said Tony Standish. "This is most uncivilized!"

Vanessa Coole then hurled herself into the action.

In the midst of the scuffling, Jack managed to turn and smile to Sarah who was backing away with Hope.

"See you upstairs?"

He saw her roll her eyes and usher Hope away in a graceful retreat.

And then he returned to the fray.

Sarah stood by Hope outside the front door of the Manor, breathing in the fresh air with relief. Out here there was only silence — not a hint of the mayhem that had just gone on inside.

"You okay?"

Hope nodded. "Just thinking — he had something most of us never have. A love that lasts a lifetime."

There was more to tell her friend about that love, and one more thing to be done, Sarah knew.

But for now...

She saw Jack emerge from the house, pulling his jacket straight. He stopped and seemed to consider.

"You know, in the end — there wasn't a murder," he said. "There was just one awful and messed up family."

"They still at it?" said Sarah.

"Oh yes. But I think Tony's got them under control now."

"Time for a cup of tea — don't you think?"

Jack pursed his lips. "Maybe, dunno—something stronger?"

And both she and Hope nodded.

"Come on," he said. "Let's head up to the village. Grab one at the Angel."

"What do you mean — one?" said Sarah.

"First round's on me," said Hope.

And the three of them headed up the gravel drive, the tall figure of Jack in the middle, their shoulders hunched in the chill afternoon wind.

A VISITOR FROM BOMBAY

A WEEK LATER and Sarah stood next to Jack, staying back a bit at the graveside of Victor Hamblyn, as their visitor took some steps forward, and placed some white lilies there.

All was quiet, with the leaves mostly gone, and winter looming.

The woman's name was Anindita. The daughter of Geeta, she had come from India to claim her inheritance after Sarah tracked her down.

After a few moments of kneeling by the grave, Anindita reached out, touched the stone, and then stood up.

"You know, all those years, with that money coming into the school's account... I wish I had known that it was him."

"I guess Victor didn't want you to feel obliged."

"Bet he felt good just knowing how much he helped," said Jack.

"And now this... inheritance."

"Tony Standish has all things arranged for you?"

She nodded. "Yes. He will act with power of attorney, arrange for the sale, take care of all the bank details. He's been wonderful."

"One of the best," Sarah said.

"So you have read the letters?" Jack asked.

"Yes. So heartbreaking. I know my mother's family would have sent them back. What my mother and Victor did, her breaking with tradition, would have been unacceptable back then. Even now such things are hard."

"It seems he stopped writing after a decade. But somehow he learned of you, and your school."

"Without him, it would have been impossible. My country has been so poor."

"And the photos of your mother with Victor," Sarah said. "Geeta — so beautiful."

Anindita did a slight bobble with her head. "Yes, she certainly was. Even when she was old, before she passed away, still such a serene and beautiful face."

"Here. Just a few old movies. The colour faded, but…"

She handed the Indian woman a disc.

Anindita took it with a smile, "Thank you."

"You'll see them together, laughing, so young. Victor in his dress whites, your mother's sari blowing in the wind. So happy."

Anindita looked at the disc.

"For such a short time. And yet, it lasted for their whole lives."

They all stood quietly as if by talking about Victor, he was somehow there with them.

But then Anindita reached out and took Sarah's hand.

"Thank you for everything." Then to Jack. "And you too, Mr Brennan."

Sarah sensed that Anindita had something to say, maybe something that she wasn't sure of.

Until…

"You know the date of the marriage certificate?"

"Yes. June. 1947," Sarah said.

Anindita smiled, then a look down to the grave.

Another bobble, the smile so warm, happy. "Perhaps you can guess."

She looked Sarah right in the eyes.

"I was born in the spring of 1948. March."

Sarah nodded.

Yes, she thought, *I had guessed as much. Nine months after Victor married his Geeta.*

Now Anindita released her hand.

"And now, I must go, so many relatives in London to visit! But thank you both for helping me come here, to pay respects to the man who helped me and my school." A deep beat. "My dear, sweet father."

And with that, Anindita said:

"I will think of you and him often!"

And Sarah took her hand as they left the graveyard.

She looked back at Jack and thought... *only the two of us could have unravelled all this.*

We're a team.

And on a cold October day, that thought made her feel warm indeed.

NEXT IN THE SERIES:

CHERRINGHAM

A COSY CRIME SERIES

MURDER BY MOONLIGHT

Matthew Costello & Neil Richards

Just two weeks to go before the Cherringham Charity Christmas Concert. Choir rehearsals are in full swing. Then the worst thing happens: Tabby Kimball, one of the singers, is found dead from a severe allergic reaction to one of the home-made rehearsal cakes. Jack is pulled in to help bolster the depleted choir - and soon he's convinced that Tabby's death was no accident. Sarah agrees, and quickly the two of them are immersed in the jealousies, rivalries and passions of Cherringham's Rotary Club choir …

ABOUT THE AUTHORS

Matthew Costello (US-based) and **Neil Richards** (UK) have been writing TV scripts together for more than twenty years. The best-selling Cherringham series is their first collaboration as fiction writers: since its first publication as ebooks and audiobooks the series has sold over a million copies.

Matthew is the author of many successful novels, including *Vacation* (2011), *Home* (2014) and *Beneath Still Waters* (1989), which was adapted by Lionsgate as a major motion picture. He has written for The Disney Channel, BBC, SyFy and has also written dozens of bestselling games including the critically acclaimed *The 7th Guest*, *Doom 3*, *Rage* and *Pirates of the Caribbean*.

Neil has worked as a producer and writer in TV and film, creating scripts for BBC, Disney, and Channel 4, and earning numerous Bafta nominations along the way. He's also written script and story for over 20 video games including *The Da Vinci Code* and *Broken Sword*.

Printed in the USA
CPSIA information can be obtained
at www.ICGtesting.com
LVHW042126171023
761014LV00089BA/1015